The Long Silence

The Long Silence

Paul Jentz

Writers Club Press
San Jose New York Lincoln Shanghai

The Long Silence

Writers Club Press
an imprint of iUniverse.com, Inc.

For information address:
iUniverse.com, Inc.
5220 S 16th, Ste. 200
Lincoln, NE 68512
www.iuniverse.com

ISBN: 0-595-16957-0

Printed in the United States of America

For Gayle

CHAPTER ONE

He could hear the jingle for the butcher shop in Seneca, then came the stock market report. It was always the same. The announcer's nasal drone of slaughter cows up a quarter, lamb down seven-eighths had always been there and would always be there, and high up on the shelf by the kitchen sink the fat white radio with fat white buttons would always be tuned to the Fargo station, WDAY, but only two other stations reached as far as Junkers, and they didn't come in very well anyway.

Jim liked to lie there, listening under the covers, dull white light seeping in around the shade, specks of dust falling through.

Her hands go into the cupboard then come out again. They go to the table then go back again. Where are her hands now?

Brown smell of toast. Black smell of coffee. There. Silverware drawer.

His father was getting his coat on to leave for work.

"So—call you about the washing machine."

"What?" Jim's mother answered.

"Said—call you about the washing machine. Fish tonight?"

"What?"

"Dinner. Fish?"

"I suppose."

"Pan's grisly here."

"Just leave already! I'll clean when I clean!"

He left.

Jim threw back the covers, swung out of bed, then crept through a long, narrow hallway to the kitchen. The broken glass globe in the ceiling there cast a blue shadow across the table and the floor; white slivers of light cut jaggedly along the walls.

He slid two pieces of bread into the toaster, pushed the lever down, then peered into the slots to watch the coils heat up and turn red. He warmed his hands over the top, observing the slow transformation from bread to toast going on inside.

He was alone at the table, just the way he wanted it. His mother was in the bedroom getting dressed. Closet doors opened and closed. Dresses slid off their hangers, then slid back on. She sang under her breath, "La la la, la la la, la la la…"

He got his knife ready with some butter, then poured a bowl of cereal and splashed in the milk and sugar. He pressed the cereal down into the milk with his spoon.

The toast popped up.

He spread it with a thick layer of creamy yellow butter, washed it down greedily with gulps of orange juice, then started on his cereal—it was soaked perfectly now, not too soggy and just crisp enough.

Coffee was beginning to perc again on the back burner, the aroma spreading throughout the kitchen; water bubbling through the glass knob on top of the pot turned from clear to brown.

"Shut the burner off." His mother's far away voice.

Jim got up and pressed one of the smooth white buttons. It was a new stove—an electric one. The buttons were all lined up on the side. He liked how they felt—tiny holes in the middle where your finger went.

In the sink next to the stove a bright silver fish—a walleye—lay spread out on a newspaper. Grandpa Sedler dropped it off, probably before the sun was up. Sometimes he'd be out casting his first line on lake Cocytus while the stars were still out; he'd always catch something, then come by on his way home. If no one was awake, he'd just leave a stringer on the porch.

"Touch it. It doesn't bite." His mother was watching from her bedroom doorway. She was still in her gown; her green eyes stared through a clay mask, dried and cracked now.

She ran a brush through her raven hair.

He glanced down at the floor, nervously smoothing his own unkempt hair. She laughed, then disappeared again and swung the door shut. He went back to his room.

He listened as she sat at her vanity—the rattle of makeup jars, a spray of perfume, then the plastic click of her eyeliner box to indicate the last touch.

She pushed her chair away.

The drape in the living room swooshed back on its rail.

Jim drew up the shade at his own window. The school was across the street. Everyone else was on the playground. It was a quarter to nine now. School started at nine. He learned how to time it so he wouldn't have to be outside with the others—he just stood there at the window, watching.

He got dressed and headed back out to the kitchen. Swapshop was on the radio. His mother was sitting at the table, drinking coffee. Her hair was tied back now, her face stark white, her lips bright red.

"You're always late."

"The bell hasn't rung yet."

"Well you're going to be late."

He put on his hat and coat, grabbed his books and left. A cold November sky arched above him, gray and sunless, and the wind made the bare tree branches clack against one another. Sparrows picked at the frozen ground.

A five-sixty tractor pulling a four bottom plow thundered down the street, black diesel pouring from the stack; Jim's uncle Will was driving. The tractor didn't have a cab, only a canvas windscreen, so he hunched himself up close against it, his chin tucked down tight into his collar. He waved to his nephew and the young Kern waved back. Bill had just finished plowing; the shiny moldboards were streaked with heavy clay. He was headed out to the farm west of town. Jim leaned against the charred black oak trunk at the edge of the driveway, watching the tractor and its black billows disappear into the country.

The school bell rang.

"Hey Jimmy girl!"

"Jimp the Chimp!"

"Hey here comes little Jimmy Wimmy!"

Chuckie Butz was the last to yell. Jim watched him spit like grown ups did. Chuckie's friends laughed and spit too.

Jim ran his finger up and down the edge of his notebook to look like he was thinking about something important. He kept his eyes on the ground as he crossed the street.

At least he didn't have to be in the same room with Chuckie, he thought. He was in the second grade so he went to Mrs. Melpo's room on the right and Chuckie was in the third grade, so he went to Mrs. White's room on the left. Further down, fifth and sixth graders went to Mrs. Black's room and seventh and eighth graders went to Miss Calli's room. Everything was squared off in twos. Four square rooms. Two times four equals eight. When you were in the eighth grade you graduated. How to get to Miss Calli's room? But Miss Calli was a fat monster whose spike heels gashed the floor wherever she walked. He liked his teacher, Mrs. Melpo, though. She was tall and thin and she had a gloomy, sad voice that seemed to come from far off.

He put his books away inside his desk and got his pencils ready for the day. He was in the row next to the window so he could look out at the trees and the fields whenever he wanted. There were four rows altogether. His grade had ten students, but the first grade had only five students.

Mrs. Melpo closed the door at the back of the room then went up to her desk. After everyone was seated she turned and faced the flag hanging in the corner above the blackboard.

That was the signal to stand and put your hand on your heart.

I pledge allegiance to…

The alphabet was strung behind a silver wire below the flag on black cardboard rectangles. They were divided into two rows: the top one cursive and the bottom one printed, but before the rectangles Jim learned his alphabet in the basement at home on the green chalkboard there. His oldest brother, Lauerence, taught it to him by holding the chalk in Jim's hand and tracing out the letters. Lauerence's hands were cold and sweaty.

It was time to get in line and go to the kitchen for milk.

They filed off through a long brick hallway, at the far end of which the ceiling sloped and the walls narrowed as if leading down into a mine. It always made Jim feel dizzy and disoriented to walk there. His legs stiffened as if they were made of wood.

The air in the kitchen was stained with a greasy yellow light, and Mrs. Archer, the cook, took up her post at the counter dispensing milk cartons and straws to each of the rosy-cheeked children. Her flabby arms shook with palsy—always worse in the morning—and her red face twisted into a drooling grimace of a smile. Her husband, Art, was the janitor. He was perched on a stool in back by the freezer, watching the milk line progress. His leg was torn off by a thresher some years ago, and the empty trouser leg was folded neatly and pinned up around the stump.

Jim opened his milk and poked in the straw. The idea was to drink it down as fast as possible and then plunk the empty carton with an expert and defiant flourish into the garbage can in the middle of the floor. Harvey Waller and Marvin Butz, Chuckie's younger brother, were always first to finish. Jim finished last, about the same time the girls did—a fact that did not spare him any ridicule from Butz and Waller and the others.

They marched back to the room, then mumbled themselves into their seats. The pens started scratching again, the girls' heads bowed to the page, the boys' heads lolling.

Jim had secreted away one of the books from the musty shelf in the back of the room. He opened it and read most of the morning.

The gaudie girlonds deck her grave,
The faded flowres her corse embrave...

That sounded nice and sad.

I"ll sit and mourn all at her grave
For a twelvemonth and a day...

That sounded nice and sad too...

The king sits in Dumferling toune,
Drinking the blude-reid wine...

Snow started to fall in hard icy flakes. Little by little the trees and fields disappeared, lost behind a gray-white screen. The snow was mixed with sleet which made a ticking sound on the window. The snow and the sleet muffled everything, not only outside the window, but in the classroom as well. Mrs. Melpo was teaching math to the first grade. The snow made her voice seem even farther away than usual. She had the students go up to the blackboard to work. The timid clicking of the chalk on the board mixed with the ticking of the sleet.

The snow made him feel warm and cozy. Doves cooed at the window, tucked away beneath the eves.

Everything seemed to pass into a dream as he looked outside and thought about the fields hidden under the cover of snow, how one field led to another and another after that. He followed them all the way to the end of the earth...But everything was still hidden, everything was underneath.

Chapter Two

He propped the atlas up by the window and knelt, tucking an afghan in tightly around his legs. He was cold and shivery. A white leafy moss of frost grew inside the panes and the wind felt like it cut straight through the glass, flowing through the icy leaves, and he could smell the cold and the frost like it was summer when everything was green, hot and living instead of white, cold and dead. It was like breathing something that was completely blank. It was also like the smell of a hidden away place, a private place, and the smell made him shiver again, not so much because he was cold but because he liked being hidden away now—everyone else was way down the hall and past the kitchen in the living room and they would leave him alone for the rest of the night with his maps—the snow and the cold just on the other side of the window, leaking through.

The wind rattled the panes; counterweights knocked in dull leaden ghost shoes. Tiny dark airless freezing shafts. You'd hear them too whenever you opened or shut the window. Thwum clun, thwum clun, thwum…And in the summertime that's where the spiders grew—between the walls—and you couldn't hear them but you knew their spider legs were ticking up and down inside because there were so many, but now they were dead, and they kept dying and piling up there because they didn't have anywhere else to go, mostly, except a few always got out and crawled up from the basement.

One day his mother killed a spider with a piece of tissue paper and then she chased him around the house with it, laughing and shrieking:

Little spider! Little spider!

She pushed the spider into his face so he could see the guts up close, laughing…

He broke off shards of frost with his fingernail and pushed them around on the glass. They left wet streaks behind.

He opened the atlas.

The places with the most jagged, rugged lines were best. He was disappointed with straight lines. North Dakota was practically all straight lines. The top line was bowed slightly, and the east edge, that was the Red River, was a little jagged, but the other two lines were exactly straight like a carpenter's square. He knew the Red River flowed north and that was supposed to be special, just like the Nile, only it wasn't the Nile and it wasn't even red; it was a muddy brown. He knew about the Nile from Catechism. Moses came down the Nile.

In North Dakota all the counties were nothing but little squares and rectangles, and then inside those were more squares because every mile there was a road and all the roads crisscrossed so everything was just little squares stacked on top of one another. It's because everything was so flat. If there were mountains and lakes you couldn't put roads every mile and you couldn't cut things up into little squares. That's what his uncle told him once when they were looking at the map of North Dakota that hung in the store. "Miles and miles of nothin' but miles and miles."

Jim didn't like the store. His father and Will owned it now; before that it was Grandpa Kern's. They sold farm equipment—International Harvester—and in back was the shop where the mechanics worked, Chuck Gast and Dell Rittmeister. He liked Chuck—he was a quiet round little man, and Dell was the cowboy—he loved to tell stories and he knew how to curse, so when he could Jim sneaked back into the shop just to listen. Grandpa Kern's first wife was Dell's aunt. She was a Schonheit. No one talked about her. She died when she was twenty. Right after that was when Grandpa went to the hospital the first time. "He'd get tired," Will explained.

Grandpa Kern started the store during the Depression; now he just sat in a blue steel chair in the corner of the office, smoking cigarettes, a yellow gnarled-up root for a hand, head crooked to the side, shirtful of ash…

That's what happened when you were old and he was always old except in the pictures of him on the wall in the office. In one of them he's standing out in the street next to the gas pumps in front of the store. His hat is tilted to the side. There is a shadow across his eyes. His suit coat is opened, but his vest is tightly buttoned. The index finger on his left hand is slightly uncurled, pointing vaguely downward. He doesn't smile. "That's when he was young as me," Will said.

So Jim tried to figure: I'm five years younger than Tip. Tip is five years younger than Lauerence. Lauerence is in high school. Tip's almost in high school. I'll be Tip's age, then Lauerence's age, then Will's age, then Grandpa's. He imagined himself sitting in his grandfather's chair, covered in ash, head bent. No, Grandpa Kern never looked up. He couldn't since the night he got trapped outside in a blizzard and his neck froze that way. If you touched it in the right spot, it would still be cold.

Tip and Lauerence slept upstairs. They had their own rooms but sometimes Tip slept in Lauerence's bed. Sometimes they'd wrestle and Tip would scream and Lauerence would scream. Then sometimes too Lauerence would tear off running, no matter how dark, and he would scream all alone.

Tip played basketball and he was the smartest in his class. He was going to be a lawyer or a doctor. Lauerence was always getting into trouble. One night he almost went to jail. He was going to be a writer. Sometimes at night he read stories to Jim in his room upstairs. Jim liked that, so he learned not to think about everything else. It was over soon, and besides, he'd make fifty cents.

He thought: what are you before you are what you are? You weren't alive, but you weren't dead either. But you were more dead than alive, because you weren't here, and if you weren't here where were you? So you had to be mostly dead, in heaven. Jim liked sitting there and watching the snow and thinking.

The rope on the school flagpole across the street made a sound like a dull icy bell. It did that in the wind, and it was especially loud in the winter because the wind was always blowing then.

The church steeple flickered in and out of view through a break in the grove. He liked how the church looked, and he liked going to mass, especially when there was a lot of incense and candles and music, though sometimes he got so dizzy he had to leave early. He was still glad that he was Catholic and he could go there instead of where Grandpa Kern, his father and Will had to go—they went way out in the country because they were Lutheran, and their church was small and wooden and it was miles away in the middle of nowhere. The Catholic church was made of brick, and it had enormous stained glass windows and an organ so big it shook the pews when it played.

Pretty soon his father would be going up town to check the store because he heard him in the kitchen now—the counter under the sink made a dull snap when he opened it and then the cabinet above the sink made a dull snap too where the glasses were.

That meant it was a little after eight. Jim taught himself how to tell time because he made a clock once. He cut it out of orange construction paper and printed all the hours in black crayon. He hooked the hands to the face with a gold fastener, then he laid down on the rug in the living room and stared up at the clock in the kitchen above the stove. When the hands there moved, he followed with his own clock until he went all the way around the dial, reciting each hour as he went.

"Gonna go up, check the store."

"And then what?"

What do you mean? Got inventory."

"Yeah, and then what?"

Two dull snaps.

Jim Kern. Jimmy. He heard his father say once: "The door was stuck so I had to jimmy it open with my knife." He heard the mechanics use the word too. To jimmy something open. Jimmy meant to break something open, and it was the thing you used to break something open. It gave him a funny feeling to hear his name used that way.

He closed the atlas and sat with his face pressed close to the window. He blew on the glass and watched it fog. He watched the fog clear then peered out into the backyard.

The streetlight cut for an instant across his father's face as he hurried off into the night, hunched over, one hand on his hat, the other holding his collar shut against the cold, unbuckled boots kicking up puffs of snow, the trail draggling down the buried walk.

Chapter Three

"Hey Arly, What'd'ya say?"

"Not much, Neb."

"Seven Seven?"

"Yeah."

"Helluva storm comin'."

"Yeah."

"Heard a foot or more."

"Could be."

Neb's black birdlike eyes darted furtively inside their black boney sockets as he fixed the drink and set it on the bar. He veered back a moment, surveying the land from somewhere high up in the clouds, his enormous bulk tottering, then, lunging downward, he scraped Arly's dollar up in a scabrous swoop of his claw.

"Keep—change, Neb."

Neb knuckled out two knocks on the bar top, gave his customary bow, a compromise between deference and disdain, then slid away to the register.

Arly felt a little drunk already from his whiskeys at home. His third now was giving him a nice edge. It felt good to be out of the store and out of the house. He needed to be alone for awhile. The place will be filling up in a little bit, that'll be all right, but now he needed to be by himself. Anna Lee said nine thirty. That'll be just right.

He tapped his Copenhangen tin, pinched off a chew then poked it home to its customary socket, bulbous now in a gristly cheek. A trickle of brown juice escaped and drained down his chin. He wiped it clean with the back of his hand.

A meaty slap fell across his back. "Arly! You sly son of a bitch! You pulled it off!"

The burnt red of Kurt Knott's face, its broken blood vessels like a glowing map of exposed nerves, was sudenly hovering there in the shadow beside him. Both Kurt and Arly backed the town council decision to buy the old St. Michael's church on mainstreet and turn it into a shed for the maintainer. Everyone agreed it was Arly's influence that swung the vote.

"Yeah, you told 'em! What they need St. Michael for anyway? Hell with that noise! Yeah, Catholics just leave their old junk to rot—Hell, they'd just let it set there a thousand years, they wouldn't care. Jesus Christ is right! What'd they need—new church for anyway? Fancy enough—bring the Pope in! Yeah. Leave the old church behind just eatin' up good tax land, all it is. Least the town can finally put it to some good now. Just freeloadin' on the tax rolls, all it is—just like you said. What they gonna do? Store all their used-up old crosses in there? They got enough of 'em. You did good, and you jewed 'em down good too. They might have made a couple bucks, but that's only fair I guess. Yeah. Musta been tough, sayin' what you said, I mean, you married to a...Oh hell, I'm sorry, Arly..."

"Just thought—best for the town."

"Well, least us Lutherans stick together. No, it just don't figure. They outnumber us like there's no tomorrow, still..."

"Don't want to talk 'bout it no more, Kurt."

"Sorry, Arly. Know I always go on too much. Hey, Nebo!"

Neb looked up from his register.

"Get this God-almighty politician here a drink! He's gettin' dry!"

Arly managed a gracious half-salute, then he watched out of the corner of his eye as Kurt disappeared again into the darkness at the end of the bar.

Tired of all this. Gotta buy him one now. Why do guys always gotta do that? Least he'll leave me alone for awhile. Tired of all this. Church shoulda been taken care of long time ago. Cause nothin' but trouble. Then I gotta get it all straight again.

Another trickle of brown juice trickled out. He wiped it, then ran his hand over a flat monkish helmet of black hair.

"Now who's this handsome man settin' here all alone?" Anna Lee came up from behind and whispered smokily into his ear. She tossed off a thick lock of brunette hair from her shoulder then ran a playful hand up and down his back.

Arly spun around on his stool, blushing. "Well—why dont—set down—I'll introduce…"

"Don't mind if I do," she drawled.

"Glad—you—came."

She winked. "You know you can count on me."

"Yeah, I know. But—sometimes things come up."

"Not yet at least."

She gave another wink, the perfect white of her teeth flashing.

He finished his drink. "Can—get you something?"

"Sure. How about a glass of Catawba?"

"Like that wine, don't you?"

"Yeah. I'm pretty much a wine girl. Sometimes a beer girl. But you know what?"

"What?"

"At least I'm *all* girl."

She slapped the bar top with the tips of her fingers. Arly laughed vaguely. He called for another round.

"How's Bob?" He asked.

"Went to Madrid this afternoon to sell some grain. He made it as far as Dick's bar. When he starts that early he don't last long."

"He at home then?"

"Well, somebody's been snoring in my bed since suppertime." She laughed, nudged Arly in the knee and winked. "Not me though. I'm rarin' to go!"

She raised her glass in a toast. "To me! I'm a wild one all right!"

Arly elevated his own glass and stammered something out in response under his breath.

"How's Nora?" Anna Lee asked.

"Home. Got—headache."

"That's too bad."

"Yeah."

"Say, you remember last year when we all went fishing on Lake Cocytus and I caught that great big walleye?"

"I remember—you—nearly capsized us!"

"Well you're the one that couldn't get my net untangled!"

"I was—busy tryin' to—reel in myself and get your net at the same time!"

"Well, you did it! I don't know how, but you netted my fish but good, and you were still reeling and reeling, then it flew up in the air…"

"That was—big one all right!"

"Then after that you got an even bigger one. . "

"Oh that! Just a skunk bullhead. Taste like mud, and the bigger they are the muddier they get."

"I still like 'em though…"

He waved his hand past his face.

She poked him in the side. "You just don't know what's good."

"Walleye's good."

She emptied her wine and ordered another round. "So how are the boys?"

"All right. Lauerence, well, we're lookin' at college up—Fargo."

"What's he want to do?"

"Don't know. Journal…Journalism."

"Gonna be a writer?"

"Yeah. I don't know."

"How about Tip?"

"Real good. Doin' real good. He's always studying, you wouldn't believe it."

"Wish mine was that way. You know, last week, just got his permit. What does he do? He gets drunk and puts the car in the ditch."

"Hurt?"

"No. Nothings gonna hurt all the rocks in his head. He's his old man all over again. Gonna get some girl pregnant in about two years and that'll be that."

She took another swallow. "You're youngest then. How's he doin'?"

"Well, tell ya. He's awful quiet. You know, his teacher, she said last year, might be—good idea—hold him back. He don't mix too well. Well, she put it, she said, he don't socialize—way he should. But his mother, she didn't want anything to do with that. I don't know. I suppose, see her point. Might have to – state school—that's not good either. But his grades – don't know what—do. If he could just get by."

"He's only a kid now. He'll grow out of it. Tomorrow's another day, and who knows, he could even grow up and be a mayor—like his old man!"

Arly laughed. "That again…"

"Well, why not? You'd be a good mayor, and I think you ought to run. A lot of people think you should. You know you'd get elected."

"Well, I might. Haven't made up—mind yet completely. Thinkin' about it."

"Gotta do more than think about it. As far as I'm concerned, you've already been elected. In fact, from here on in, I'm calling you Mr. Mayor, and I'm gonna be your campaign manager! A vote for Arly Kern is a vote for, for early corn!"

"You…"

The juke box erupted in twangy cascades:

If I had a dollar

For every kiss you gave away…

"C'mon boys, gonna take *all* your money tonight!" The shrill cadence of Lucy Fern's voice razored through the smoky room as she gathered her poker minions at the corner table by the front window, just behind Arly and Anna Lee. The two of them turned for a moment to watch as the usual players crept out of their booths and descended from their stools.

And as the congregation took shape around the ritual deck, Lucy's purple cheeks fluttered and her fat arms flailed at the air. "C'mon boys! C'mon boys…"

One of the players, Frankie Faulheit, had been sitting at the table for some time already. Drowned in sleep, as usual, he could barely hold up his head, and his arms shook as if he suffered from a perpetual fever. Swaggering toward him, Harv Veilfrab spilled a handfull of peanuts into his mouth and washed it down with the last of his Grain Belt, the Adam's apple in his crane-like neck clicking. In spite of the scrawny neck, pencil arms and pencil legs, his belly forever displayed a seventh month stage of pregnancy. He belched and wiped the sweat from his forhead repeatedly as he re-aranged the chairs beside Frankie, clearing enough room to sit. Next to Harv, Charlie Wallust took up his own usual place, running his fingers through a scraggly goat-like beard. His colorless eyes were only staring white spots fixed beside a long, thin, constantly dripping nose, the tip of which he wiped clean with his finger between alternate strokes of his beard. Already counting out his money as he scraped his game leg across the floor, Gary Geiz picked out the greasy quarters and dimes hidden in forgotten pockets of the filthy rag he wore for a coat. He sat next to Ben Eiden, a black-toothed, shrivelled little man whose lips and chin bore the permanent stains from a lifetime of dribbling tobacco juice; he grimaced as he eyed the money in his neighbor's yellow hand, then his eyes moving slowly around the table registering everyone's strengths and weaknesses, his tongue darting snakelike between his razor lips, he squeezed his hands together, keeping a special eye on Lucy as she shuffled the deck in a rhinestone blur. The last one to be seated was a red-faced, perpetually scowling man who went only by his last name, Grimm. Grimm spent three years in prison for assault. He came back to Junkers right after his release; he did odd jobs now, and he hired himself out to farmers in the area as a fieldhand. His nickname was "The Grimm Reaper." A lot of people took pity on him. After all, his father was a drunk who lived in a shed down by the railroad tracks. That's gotta be tough. Sometimes he even talked about how sorry he was for the things he'd done.

The floor around the table was littered with nut shells, cigarette butts, and sticky pools of black slush and spilled drinks. The players mumbled into their places with the routine insults and boasts, then settled down to business.

Yes if I had a dollar
For every kiss you gave away,
I'd spend it on a coffin
For delivery today.

Anna Lee drained her glass. "There they go again."

"Yeap. Don't know how—do it. Every night. Well, they're good guys. You know, well, Charlie there, Wally we call him, he's—real good guy. I get along with him real good. Pays his bills. Used to go fishing with him. Still do."

"They're quite a bunch all right. They're just the boys. Gotta do something around here, might as well play cards. Go crazy otherwise. I don't know. I wish I could just…Oh hell, I just feel so damn drab all the time."

"You're not drab. You're—pretty."

"No. I'm as drab as the night is long."

"Shouldn't say that."

"Why not? It's true. You know I had a birthday last week."

"Well, happy birthday."

She laughed with a tiny brittle smile. "That makes me near as old as you. When's your birthday anyway?"

"Next month. Twenty-second. I don't think much about it."

"Well, it's different with men. When a woman gets old, the only thing she's good for is the boneyard."

"Just shouldn't say…"

"Arly! Sonunumbitch! Hardes' workin' man—town! Whadya say?" Irv Schlotzz's voice dieseled in as he backed himself between their stools and slammed his empty Grain belt on the bar. "Gonna buy you—drink!"

"No, 'cause I—gonna buy *you* one!"

"Oh no, Ar…"

"Your money's no good here, Irv!"

"You old sonunumbith you!" He laughed, igniting a cigarette in his cupped hands. "So, Analee! Where's old man?"

"Sawin' wood in the shed, just didn't want to quit."

"Farms a tweny four hourday business. Better believe—I know! He's—good man!"

He hoisted a fresh Grain Belt. "Say, Arly. Them hogs your brother says, needs shippin', tell 'im, jus' give me—call. End—the week be good. I'm shipin' cattle for Healy 'till then."

"All right Irv."

Whipping his beer around in a broad salute, he backed away and headed off into the crowd.

Lucy choked out a shrill rattling laugh. "You boys are just my type!" She gathered her winnings in a flabby rhinestone sweep. "Just my type…"

"So, mayor, are you going to allow gambling in your new administration?"

"Don't know. Kinda fun watchin'."

Arly filled a meditative pause with a pinch of snuff.

"Maybe not such—bad idea."

"What?"

"Runnin'."

"That's what I've been telling you."

"Wish Nora..."

"What?"

"Said I. I just wish to hell..."

She looked at him without speaking.

"I wish to hell Nora would say that."

"What do you mean?"

"I think she takes me for granted a lot."

"Well maybe she's used to finer things than little old Junkers can dish out. If you ask me...No...I'm sorry I said...I mean, she's my friend. It's hard for both of you."

She traced the rim of her glass with her finger. "Neb!" She called out. Liven it up down here!"

Neb splashed out another glass of wine while he balanced an upended Seagram's bottle in his open palm.

"He sure likes—show off, don't he?"

"Sure does. Will you look at all these people? Everyone in the whole county's here."

"Yeah, well, you know, gonna be—polka band later—Guernsey Brothers."

"Yeah?"

"They got quite a following. Play all around here."

"Maybe we could play all around here too..."

Arly glanced to the side. Nobody was watching.

"I left the car running." She slid her purse inside her coat. "You know, the cold...better check it."

"Need any help?"

"If I'm not back in five minutes..."

She left. Arly took his time finishing his drink—he felt drunk but at the same time his head felt clear—then he picked up his hat and left. The car was just around the corner by the butcher shop.

Neb leaned over the bar to Art Blake and jabbed his thumb at the door. "How she do it?"

Art drew his mouth back in a perverse smile and licked his lips. "*Anal* Lee. How else?"

Sly laughter erupted as they slapped the bar top and shook their heads.

The Guernsey Brothers were hard at it by the time Arly and Anna Lee got back.

"You go—sit down," Arly said, pointing to an empty booth. "I'll get—drinks."

He inched his way through the crowd and squeazed up to the bar next to Art. Art was the blacksmith. He was a huge man, and his left arm bore the blue smear of an antique sailor's tattoo—a blotchy sun rising above an anchor with a snake wrapped around it. Underneath was a woman's name, "Chery." He was talking to Stubby Beadman, who ran the Farmer's Elevator in town.

"Got family comin' in from all around the state, and a twenty four pound bird to feed 'em!" Stubby said.

"You put 'em up at the house then too?"

"Sleepin' wall to wall. But they're all good people—give any of 'em the shirt off my back. Yeah, it's a big time for us—last year you know, even had Grimm there come over—his old man disappeared again so he was all alone, well, felt good to do it. That was the year Charlie got killed. Good friend, thought he was gonna pull through too, then just turned for the worse. Still had his wife and kids over, had a good talk with her about it all, so that was all quite the time."

"Yeah. Holidays. Sure got the weather for it." Art turned to Arly who was still waiting for Neb to come by. "Thought you took off, Arly."

"Went across street—Maurice's—little bit."

"What's happening over there?"

"Nothin' much. Hey Neb! Seven-Seven. Wine."

"Got plans for the holidays?"

"Little bit. Usual."

"Nora's folks, they come over Christmas usually, don't they?"

"Yeah."

Stubby leaned back on his stool. "Well, you want there, Arly, stop by Thanksgiving, you and Nora. Bring the boys too."

"Nah. We got—gonna—her folks over then too."

"Hell! Bring 'em with! Ain't seen George since I don't know how long. How's he doin?"

"Got the horses. Keeps busy."

"He was always the horseman. Every horse my dad bought, he got it from George. That's the way it was for most every one around here too."

Neb brought the drinks. Arly muttered good-by and left.

Anna Lee snapped her compact shut and raised her glass. "Thought you'd never make it back."

"Talkin' to Stubby, Art."

"What do they have to say?"

"Just holidays. Don't know how Stubby does it. Those big feeds he puts on."

"That's what he's famous for."

"Lotta trouble."

"Yeah, he likes it though. He's that kinda guy. Up at the church you know, he's always doing someting. Not many people like that."

"No—suppose not. Does—good job up at—elevator, I know that."

"That's right. That's right, he does. Takes all kinds, Arly."

"Suppose."

She tipped her wine up in a toast. "To all kinds. Yeah. Some good, some real losers. I reckon Bob's turnin' over in his bed about now, wonderin' where the hell he is. You know he walks in his sleep?"

"Yeah, you told me that once."

That must be something. How can you be asleep and walking at the same time? Of course, with him, that's the way he does everything." She threw her head back and laughed with all her teeth. "Who the hell can tell the difference!"

Arly laughed nervously.

It was midnight by the time he got home.

Nora was asleep. The only sound in the house was the wind and the snow slamming in muffled blasts against the windows and the walls. Without taking off his coat, he crept off to the living room with his Seagrams and turned on the television, but all the stations were off the air. He poured himself a drink and settled back in his chair. He set the bottle on the floor behind the magazine rack.

Have to get—bucker out tomorrow. Gettin' pretty deep. Hard on animals. Market's good. Tell Bill call Irv. Get them hogs out Friday. Yeah. Old Bob. Drunk all the time. Own damn fault. Gonna lose—whole farm don't wake up. Yeah, that's right though. Really ain't his fault he's slow. Took a bad hit in the war. I got lucky I guess. Shore patrol. All we ever killed—that whale. Bored. Blood all over the water. Belly gunner started it. Hawksaw—Hawksawyer—no, Hawkshaw. "That's the one."

The unexpected eruption of his own voice startled him, then, recovering, he nodded his head, silently congratulating himself for the accuracy of the name. He finished his drink and poured himself another.

He looked around the living room. Nora's black desk in the corner was covered with books and papers. Church books, he called them, but never to her face. It was a private term. "Don't make sense," he muttered under his breath.

He tried to make out the titles of the books on her shelf. "Ain't even English, most of 'em," he mumbled, defeated. Just church. Catholic this, Catholic that. Then she bitches. Tired of it. Tired—whole damn thing.

She's Catholic too, but she's different. Ain't so big about it. Confession, all that.

He had a few more drinks, then his eyes started to close, and just when he was about to get up and go to bed, he fell asleep in his chair.

A few hours later, an especially strong blast shook the house and startled him awake. His glass was still in his hand. He got up and drew back the drape to look outside. The town was bathed in a dark blue light;

snow swirled through it in ragged blows, seeding the frozen waste with yet another winter. Vast white shapes loomed up out of the deep. He pulled his coat close around him and stared into the gloom.

Chapter Four

There was no getting around it—they had to leave the house. It had been cold enough the last two days—afraid of burning out the furnace, Arly liked to keep the thermostat turned low in a storm—but the snow and ice had taken its toll. All lines were down, and the last news on the radio before it went dead was the weather wouldn't break for at least two more days.

Arly mumbled over his coffee that morning, "If 'lectricity goes, go up —Morsch's. Wood stove there," meaning Morsch's Cafe, where half the town was already encamped.

Nora and Jim were the only ones in the house. Lauerence and Tip were stranded at their grandparent's in Weed. Grandma Sedler called at noon—Grandpa and the boys were out in the barn with the horses. He bought them a couple new saddles. The snow was just as bad in Weed, it sounded like.

Nora stood at the back window for some time before leaving, looking out at the dark winter afternoon, all the winters before and all those yet to come. It was a white wasteland without light and without end. There was nothing else to do.

She thought, if only for a minute, how easy it would be to walk away. After the storm, get in the car and leave, go to Fargo and stay with Vivian, her old girlfriend from business college, get her job back at the bank, go to school again, but this time for interior decorating. Yes. A suicide hung from every rafter.

She pulled her son's gloves tight, readjusted his scarf and pulled on her own gloves. She had surprised herself.

She smiled at Jim. "Are you ready?"

Jim nodded.

The door was frozen in its frame. She shoved until it gave way with an icy crack. She took her son's hand to guide him up over the drifts, but at the top of the first ridge the wind took her breath away and she involuntarily dropped his hand as she fought in a panic for air—tucking her chin down tight into her coat collar, covering her mouth and nose with her hands. He fell back against the door; still gasping, she scrambled down the bank after him, helped him up, then pulled him close to her side. She tried to say something, but she still didn't have enough breath to get any words out.

They inched along, and when they made it only as far as the old well in the middle of her garden she already felt like giving up, but at least she was able to breathe again, and when they reached the willow tree by the garden gate she turned to say something to Jim, but now the wind tore her words away. Jim shrugged his shoulders in response. The willow vines lashed across their faces and they moved on.

Across the road, white squalls tore through the field around Mat Rose's barn. In turns, the barn veered out of sight, then suddenly hauled up in front of them again, a hulking red slab, its warping walls straining and creaking, almost ready to careen over, then disappearing again into the storm.

Mat used to keep a few horses and a donkey in the barn, then he got sick and had to give them up. Every once in a while you'd hear him inside, muttering to himself, feeding imaginary animals.

Across from the barn the roof of John Coke's shack just broke the surface above the drifts. A dull yellow light glowed in his window. Even though the shack had been fixed up with electricity when it was still a chicken coop, all he ever used for light was a kerosene lantern. He burned coal in his stove and his toilet was a bucket with a lid on top. People wouldn't see him for months at a time. He could wait out any storm just sitting at his table, staring through a grimy yellow window.

Tugging Jim along behind and stuggling for every step, Nora was barely able to keep her balance in the shifting snow and the slick ice underneath. She began to wonder if they'd ever make it. It was just too cold. The storm was too much. She cried and was glad—it was so easy now. The tears froze on her face. It was impossible to hear her in the wind. The storm was the perfect disguise.

Gray, snow-shouldering houses like whales in a white frozen sea heaved their backs up through the ice, their smoky spumes torn away in the wind. All around the drifts rose and fell; the two of them trudged on, the storm and their breathing the only sounds they could hear until they edged past the blacksmith's shop and the howling wind was momentarily punctuated by the clanking of Art Blake's hammer. Inside, the coals burned red in his forge, and the sweat rolled down his bare arms, but from the outside, its patched and re-patched walls, and the spine of the roof cracked, the shop was like a blackened carcass tossed up cold and dead by the storm.

Across from the blacksmith's, the vaulted doors of the lumberyard snapped back on their hinges like whips exploding. Pallets of raw lumber lay scatterd in the snow; icycles hung in thick shaggy rows from the eves. Last summer, Joe Rikitz, the owner, had a heart attack while he was up shingling the roof. It was 104 degrees that day; people figure he laid up there most of the afternoon, dead. His face was blistered and cracked like a piece of drought land. It had red trickles coursing through it, and his eyes had already been pecked out by ravens.

They cut through the alley and crossed the lot between Bill Gaugn's grocery store and Morsch's Cafe. A canopy of oak trees there rose above them and they were cocooned from the storm in a still, windless canyon—in front of them the blizzard raged across mainstreet and behind them the lumberyard doors banged away idiotically, but for a while they were separate from both worlds. Nora's hands went to her face, then she pressed her fists together in angry prayer. The storm rose up around them in leviathan menace, all the mysteries of time and space moving with arctic authority above the congealed waves.

She took Jim's hand again. They felt blindly along the side of the cafe until they found the front and climbed the buried steps.

In his office at the other end of mainstreet, Arly hunched over a pile of papers at his desk; across from him, his mother penciled row after row of figures into the ledger at her old rolltop; in the corner by the safe, Grandpa Kern sat smoking cigarettes in his blue chair, his head bent to the side, his hands shaking.

Deadening all other sounds was the muffled roar of a tractor, its throttle wide open, powering an emergency generator in a snowbank outside the store. Patches of heat pumped intermittantly through the hole in the office ceiling that served as a furnace vent, but the blasts did nothing to warm the room—they merely intensified the chill. The only other weapon in their arsenal against the cold was a rusted out tin space heater beside Arly's desk; it glowed a fierce red, making a promise of warmth it could never keep. Even the tiny paper punches that fell into it from Arly's desk were in no danger of igniting.

"Where's that Abel contract?" Arly asked.

"Seed contract?"

"Well yeah. Where is it?"

"In the file with the others, I suppose."

"Ain't in there—looked."

"I don't know then."

"You put it someplace?"

"I haven't touched it."

"Well it ain't here. Where is it then?"

I don't know."

You finish that Pence account yet?"

"Just got to it."

"You better get—finished. Gotta get—statement in the mail today."

"Mail ain't going anywhere today."

"I don't care about that! Get—postmarked at least."

"Isn't even worth sending if you ask me. He never pays his bill here anyway. You just let him keep charging and charging…"

"None of your business! Just keep—books straight! Now where's Mocha? Dick Mocha – where is he – where's the file?"

"You been after him – don't know how long."

"I'll get him – none of your business! I'll get him!"

Grandma Kern wet her finger and turned the page, then she took the pencil between her teeth like a horse's bit and studied the numbers. "Just keep charging and charging…"

"Enough already!"

Grandpa Kern dropped another cigarette butt to the floor. The tips of his fingers sketched a palsied scrawl in the air, tracing the same indecipherable pattern there over and over. Smoke lingered at his ashen lips.

The wind tore the door from Nora's hand; Jim jumped inside while she struggled to keep her balance and catch the door again at the same time. It was an impossible task. When she finally got both hands on it and managed to slam it shut behind her, she stood, breathless, stunned by the steamy warmth and sudden silence of the room.

A half-dozen sets of eyes peered at her from out of the darkness, and the heavy gloom gave up a few scatterd hellos, but soon the few curious who had turned, turned back again, retracing mumbled bits of conversation, drawing their cigarettes, cigars and pipes back to life.

Matt and Glattuce Verlust were in the booth next to the door. Glattuce's rat-like face glanced up with a pinched, feeble smile for Nora, then she met her husband's eye that had been tracking her own, hovering there coal black and cold behind fat rings of cigar smoke and thick ashen whiskers. She crouched back down into her knitting.

Nora pointed her son toward an empty stool at the counter. He was only vaguely aware of her hand on his shoulder as he stood there tugging at the buttons on his coat, trying to make his thick, numb fingers work.

He peered through the smoke into a hazy black tunnel lined with sullen, unsmiling faces: farmers and farmers wives, coat collars pulled up tight, some eyes staring at fixed points in space, others cast down at the floor. Dirty puddles gathered there under the tables and the chairs, then trickled into ever-widening pools where the linoleum sagged from the rotten planks underneath.

He climbed up on the empty stool next to Carl Konig. He recognized Carl because he had a patch over one eye, so he stood out and he didn't look like everyone else. Behind the counter Mrs. Morsch flipped a ragged pile of hash browns, then poured oil over them from a can with a long curved beak like some exotic bird, her short fat fingers constantly dabbing at the black scab on her cheek as she worked.

Her whole face was a doughlike thing suspended above cookie jars and vats of grease; it presided with eyes that took in everything, translating the inexpressible into something equally inexpressible inside.

"Look at this," she said, eyeing Jim. "It's the Kern baby! Look at this now! Aren't you a little doll all bundled up! You're mother here? Of course she is."

Carl lit a cigarette and flicked the burnt match to the floor. "Baby? Ain't no baby, are you, Butch? You're Arly's boy, right?"

"Yes."

"So that means George Sedler, that's your Grandfather."

Jim nodded.

"Him and my dad, neighbors, back…" His words drifted off as he searched for something through pocket after pocket in his coat, revisiting each of them three or four times. He finally gave up and, having nothing to show for his labors, only stared at his empty, swollen hands and continued speaking. "He used to tell stories about your grandpa. I remember that. Lotta stories. This and that. His homeplace there was up on a little hill. You been there. Pretty soon…One day this fellow comes up to the door, sellin'seed. Your grandpa he's leadin' him on—gonna buy couple hundred bushels. Tells the salesman that his neighbor, that's my dad then, probably interested too…"

"Carl, miserable son of a bitch." A gray, cobweb voice interrupted from further down the counter. "Got that deal worked out up at Ketchiter's?"

"Yeah. Mostly."

"And what are you tellin' that boy anyway?"

"What are you talkin' about?"

The man with the cobweb voice waved his hand past his face in response.

Mrs. Morsch set a cup of hot chocolate down in front of Jim. He pulled the mug close, waiting for Carl to finish the story, but all he did was light another cigarette and stare off through the smoke without another word.

Jim ran his finger along the gnawed edge of the counter, a brailled legacy of a hundred years of coffee and hamburgers. He slid his palm over the scratches and gouges in the counter top itself, dabbing his fingertips into the blackened scars —another script.

"Yeeah, She comin' down all right! She sure is comin' down!" Polycarp Moulsouf's twisting barbed wire voice stung the air . He settled back next to the stove then dug out a blackened leather pouch and a gnarly pipe from his bib overalls. He gave the pipe a sharp crack on the flue.

A blue flame glowed in his cupped hands.

"Don't matter none though. Got Hell comin' out both ends!" After a moment's meditation he added, "Man's gotta eat, that's all I know. Devil comes up, world just keeps right on spinnin'!"

Polycarps's philosophy was broadcast to no one in particular. He spoke staring straight ahead, the smoke from his pipe ascending. "Take your choice —air fulla grasshoppers, mosquitoes drinkin' your blood, or *this.* He gestured with his pipe toward the white window. "Man's gotta eat, that's all I know."

Jim nudged himself around for a look at Polycarp. Only a gray impression of his face remained in the smoky shadows as he slid back out of view behind the stove, though his chortling and snickering still hung like something palpable in the air.

Nora put her hand on her son's shoulder.

"Are you hungry?"

He looked down at his fingers. She laughed and nudged him playfully. "We're going to be here for a long time, so you might as well eat something."

He looked up at her. "A hamburger?"

"You have to have more than a hamburger."

"French fries?"

"You…Ish…" Nora chided Jim. "Well, if that's what you want…"

He glanced at his mother's green eyes: for an instant, the only points of light in the dark smoke surrounding them.

She drifted back through the murmurings and the shadows and sat down at a table with three other women. They were talking about the old priest before Father Misere—Father Erfrieren. He died last fall. He was buried out in the cemetery under an altar made out of stone. There was a button on the altar, and if you pushed it the stones would move and you could see his bones.

It was getting even darker now in the room. Wind slammed against the walls; the place shook and creaked like an old ship. He tried to pick out conversations but everything he heard was garbled and hazy.

Mrs. Morsch set the hamburger down in front of him. It was on a green plate with three pickles and a pile of french fries. The plate itself was covered with fine black crosshatchings from knife and fork scrapes. He set the pickle rounds carefully on the hamburger, then poured ketchup over it and pressed the top of the bun down until the ketchup and the grease squeezed out over the sides.

It was twilight now. The storm still hadn't let up. A dark green light cast the room into a dreamlike glow. He could easlily pretend now that he was someplace else, not Junkers, not Askenazi County, not North Dakota.

The spectral figure of his father appeared in the doorway.

Nora glanced up at him over the top of the booth. He walked up to her.

He looked small and dirty. He stomped the snow from his boots.

"Closed the store early."

"So are we going to have any heat?"

"Yeah. Gonna pull—generator up with a tractor from the shop. Plug it in at the house—run a line out. Won't need it in the store anymore. Yeah. No one comin' in today anymore anyway."

Jim picked at the rest of his meal. When he finished the three of them left. It was completely dark. As they inched their way home in the pickup the snow hung like a whorling ghost, a vast milky mass shifting and glistening in the black empty November waste. No one spoke. The dim glare of the headlights only intensified the darkness and the cold as they cut their pitiful swath through the lightless town.

Chapter Five

Leaving three feet of snow in its wake, the blizzard blew itself out around noon the next day; the sudden dead calm was filled with glittering ice crystals falling through the air like diamond dust. The sun blossomed cold and yellow. Circling it sun dogs prophesied a long bitter cold spell to come. Nora looked up at them from the living room window, its stark white cretonne curtain framing the stark white waste.

The electricity came back in the night, but it was still freezing cold in the house, and as she gazed across the buried homes and tortuous drifts she rubbed her hands together, trying to warm them; even though she was wrapped in two sweaters, there seemed no escape from the chill: it went straight to the marrow and stayed there.

She remembered yesterday and the thought of leaving. She could just wish herself away…She made a mistake.

White glittering caverns, twisted gleaming slopes: a blinding landscape stretched across the fields to the horizon. There was nothing else.

Arly said he'd take her up to Fargo tomorrow to do some Christmas shopping. There was that at least. For a day she could pretend she was still living her life there so she could dress fashionably and people would look at her and think how pretty she was. Of course she'd still live downtown, or close to it, and she'd have coffee in the afternoon with her friends at the Powers with the white tablecloths, chandeliers, and a flower at every table. At night she'd be able to see a movie if she wanted, and then the lights downtown, the bright neon, flashing marquees...

After high school in Weed she lived there above Roberts Street for two years while she went to Northern Business College. Almost every night she'd go prowling with her roommate, Vivian, to look over the young men, especially the ones home on leave. Vivian still lived in Fargo. They'd be getting together tomorrow. She married money *and* class. But as much as Nora looked forward to such infrequent visits, it took its toll for days after. Even the cheap delights must be bought and paid for.

She looked down at her hands. They were chapped and red. She had to stop thinking about it. It was always worse in the winter too. She knew she had to get her mind off things, so she got her pans and measuring cups out and went to work making bread, letting the afternoon slip away as she labored over her floured counters.

At four o'clock she sat down to watch her favorite television show, Party Line. Verna Newall and Boyd Christenson were the hosts. Pat Kelly played the organ. She loved the way Verna Newall dressed, and Boyd was always making jokes. Pat Kelly seemed to know every song in the world. The show came from Fargo on WDAY. They were always talking about things that were going on there. Since it was nearly the holidays now they had quite a few school and church choirs. Nora liked the music. It was a pleasant way to end the afternoon.

As the sun set and the windows were filled with black night instead of an endless vista of freezing white, she was able to look forward to the next day with pleasant anticipation and no longer felt the old dread.

They drove to Fargo in the implement truck—Arly had to pick up a new cornhead at the International Harvester warehouse there. He'd drop Nora off downtown then pick her up again when he was done.

Hat pulled down tight to the tip of his nose, he crouched over the steering wheel as if trying to get as close to the road as possible. Nora stared out the passenger window at all the farmyards swallowed in white, snow blowers working in the driveways, farmers trying to dig out as much as possible before the next bad blow.

The truck cab rattled and shook: every rivet about to pop, every bolt about to snap.

"So, what you gonna do?" Arly shouted above the din.

"What?"

"Downtown. What you gonna—downtown?"

"See Vivian, I suppose."

"What else?"

"I don't know. Shopping."

"Gonna be busy."

"What?"

"Stores. Gonna be crowded."

"Yeah. I suppose. It's Christmas."

She glanced over at her husband's red nose, his unshaven face, and the knob in his cheek his Copenhagen called home. Her eyes closed in disgust and she turned away again to watch the farmyards passing by, the curl of smoke from the chimneys, the endless white.

"So what—what she doin'?"

"What?"

"Vi—Vivian. What she doin'?"

"She just got back from Africa."

"Africa? Wha…Never seen a nigger before?"

"She wanted to see Zebras."

"What?"

"She told Mike she wanted to see a field of Zebras in Africa, So he took her there."

"Must be nice. Suppose that's what you want—do now." He laughed.

"What's the point in asking?"

The noise in the cab provided a convenient buffer between themselves and their silence for the rest of the trip.

It was exactly one hour from Junkers to the outskirts of Fargo, and as the old landmarks came into view, especially the Starlight and The Buenos Aires just off Highway 81, she was already tapping the door handle, as much from anticipation as from nerves—The truck was a long, rumbling monster, difficult even for a professional driver, and Arly navigated with a bumpkin timidity that infuriated Nora. As they scuffled along the crowded streets it was all she could do to keep her comments to herself and respond with guarded monosyllables to his nervous litany, "Look—there! Anything? Anything comin'? What about there? Lane Clear? That the street? Clear? Look over there…"

He took advantage of a red light to drop her on Main and Roberts, just down from The Dutch Maid. The light turned as she jumped from the running board to the street, and he was already letting out the clutch as she reached up and slammed the door, the "got—gotta go!" he bit off still ringing in her ears as the monstrous rusting beast shuddered away and disappeared.

Her eyes went immediately to the old familiar doorways and signs. The music shop on the corner? Good. Still there. Little man behind the counter with the cigarette. A few steps further. That was the window. Flowers on the sill in the summertime. Who lives there now? That's me.

She had until six. He'd pick her up at the Gardner, the truck double-parked, its hazard lights apologizing to some gloomy backstreet with their tired yellow blinking, but until then…She had until six.

Nora's first stop was the Powers to meet Vivian. She asked for a window seat, and as the hostess led her through the maze of mahogany tables and purple wingbacks she undid her coat letting in the welcoming warmth of the room, the last wisps of the cold slipping away through the buttonholes. Smiling and nodding politely, the hostess took the coat from her, folded it neatly over her arm, and seated her in a comfortable nook with a full view of the street.

The train had just pulled into the station across the way. Very faintly Nora could feel its diesel throbbing through the floor. She watched, entranced, as the platform filled with disembarking passengers, their breath rising white in the air, their eyes blinking, tearing up already from the cold, searching the waiting crowd for familiar faces…

She wore a short red blazer over a white silk blouse. The buttons on the blazer were embossed with tiny ship's anchors. Her skirt was also red, cut just above the knee according to the new fashion; also, newly fashionable were her high black boots. She wore her hair down, swept back from her shoulders like a shiny wing. A pair of white gloves lay folded neatly beside her on the table.

She was aware of certain approving glances from around the room. Her finger played lightly at one of her gold buttons. She smoothed her jacket and her skirt, then took a sip of coffee from the blue china cup the waiter had just delivered. It was enough just to sit there. She looked down at her finely manicured fingers and the red nails. She spent all night working on them.

"Emmy!" Called out a soft voice from over the diners—it was Vivian, waving prettily as she strolled across the lush carpets and came up to the table. Emmy was a pet name from Nora's middle name, Emma.

Nora's face brightened and she stood to embrace her friend.

"What a doll you are!" Vivian said. "Turn around, let's take a look at you! Oh my!"

"You think so? I feel like an old cow."

Vivian winced. "Old cow? Hardly."

"Old Nellie, Nice Nellie…"

"Stop it now!"

"Mooo…"

Vivian laughed and held up a scolding finger, then threw a shock of blonde hair back over her shoulder as she sank luxuriously into the purple velvet chair. Her snow white skin was in stark contrast to Nora's dark complexion, but her eyes were the same clear, piercing green.

"So, what's this cow business all about?" Vivian asked, setting her white gloves beside Nora's.

"Oh…Nothing."

"Nothing, nothing…You should be up here where you belong. That's the answer."

"I think about it."

"And for how long now?"

Nora shrugged her shoulder in response.

"Emmy…What are you going to do?"

"I've become quite religious."

"That's not an answer."

"Things change. It's not so bad really."

"No reason to bury yourself."

The waiter appeared and took their order—sirloin tips and asparagus, "And two Drambuie," Vivian added.

The waiter left. They settled back and sipped their coffee, drifting into small talk—shopping, a party Vivian was planning.

"And the boys, how are they?"

"Lauerence is still headed for college as far as I can tell. He gets so wild sometimes, I don't know…Tip though, he starts high school next year—straight A's. You've never seen anyone study like he does."

"And your youngest?"

Nora winced. "His teacher says he has trouble learning. We might have to send him someplace. I don't know."

"That's too bad."

"Well, he was a breech baby. Backwards."

Vivian's eyes widened.

"He's so withdrawn, and it doesn't seem like he can concentrate on anything. Sometimes I get so mad at him…Lauerence reads to him a lot. That can't hurt."

When their dinners came they ate slowly, enjoying the food—the meat done perfectly, the asparagus surprisingly fresh for the middle of winter.

The waiter cleared the table. They settled back to enjoy their drinks.

"So," Vivian said. "Are you going to tell me?"

"What?"

"The story about what's going on, that's what."

"It's just…" Nora stopped herself, then turned to look outside: Christmas shoppers, packages tucked under their arms, collars pulled up, their breath rising white; the train's deep diesel panting like some fabulous silver beast, exhausted now, shaggy with ice, but ready to take off again any minute, the platform clearing…

Vivian waited.

Nora drew even further away, searching the street now with her eyes, following the courses of passersby, watching how the cars scudded through the snowy street. "The worst part is…" she started, then drifted off.

She watched out the window now passively like a helpless animal, imagining that she saw in the shape of some anonymous figure the agent of her delivery, but as her thoughts drifted from one desperate scenario to the next, she knew she was helpless against her own paralysis to follow any of them.

"I can accept everything. I have to."

Her audience still waited, hiding impatience behind slow sips from her drink.

"We have two friends," Nora said. "Another couple. Anna Lee and Bob. Bob is a little slow. He drinks more than most. But the four of us get together sometimes. Sometimes we go fishing. Sometimes we go up to the bar. Sometimes it's just Arly and Anna Lee that go up to the bar. He says he's going up to check the store at night. It's a small town. They're not fooling anyone."

"What are you going to do?"

"Nothing." She threw a loose shock of hair over her shoulder. "Better her than me."

Vivian ordered another round.

"You're lucky, Vivian," Nora said when the drinks came. "You work in a bank with a nice big office. No children. The fact is. I know what I have to do, and I'm not going to do it."

Vivian ran her finger around the edge of her glass. She studied her friend for a moment then took a drink. "I don't think you know what you're saying."

"I know it's not right, but I don't really know what *is* right. If I knew the answer, well, if I knew the answer to any of this I'd be a lot better off. Sometimes I think it's all so simple – what I could do, the next step, but then it always gets so complicated the more I think about it. You see, if I could just stop thinking about it, then everything would be all right. At least I have you to talk to though, without you, I'd be…"

"Stop."

Nora's eyes widened, her heart beating fast.

"I'm moving, Nora. We're going west. We're going to San Francisco."

She continued with a few more halting sentences. "We've been talking about it for years, Daydreaming. Then …Well…One day Mike made some phone calls…"

Nora was completely unaware of the rest of her words.

"I knew this was going to be hard on you, and I should have told you earlier this might happen."

Nora pretended to be very happy for her friend, though it was impossible and they both knew it.

"But I don't really have anyone else."

"That's all the more reason for you to pick up and…"

"I'm not going to 'pick up and' anything."

Vivian took a long swallow from her drink. "So should I believe you?"

"Believe what you want."

Her tone was sharper than she planned, but she let it go and tipped her glass up in a toast. "To me."

The rest of the afternoon they poked through their favorite shops, careful to evade the wrong subjects, and for the most part Nora felt herself free to be back in her old world. It was simple enough to pick up where her old memories had left her.

The streetlights flickered to life. It was time to head for the Gardener. Arly would be coming for her soon to take her home.

They sat among their packages, chatting over cocktails. Nora drifted pleasantly away as she watched all the activity—people picking up their keys from the front desk, walking up the marble stairway that wound in wide leisurely curves three floors through the center of the hotel. Crystal chandeliers, the uniformed waiters and bellhops…

Then it was only a matter of disbelieving the stammering unshaven figure that had slid up beside her was her husband: the awkward goodbye, his thumb jabbing the air, a last glance at her friend…

She kept rubbing the frost off the inside of the passenger window, keeping a tiny porthole open so she could look back at the fading lights of the city. She saw again in her mind the figures of those travelers on the platform, then their backs as they walked away eluding her even as she felt herself drawing toward them, merging with them; but they would remain only a forever receding mass which she could not join.

Arly coughed, wiped something off of his mouth with his hand, then sneaked another pinch of snuff into his cheek. On the way home now he bent even closer to the wheel, fighting it to keep the truck on the road: the bed was loaded with red wooden pallets full of parts for the cornhead, they were battened down with chains and ropes, and in the middle of it all rose the cornhead itself—its gleaming red fingers reaching gigantically into the sky, scooping the night wind like an armoured sail.

She looked up at the pale moon wandering companionless in the heavens. It was a long bitter cold to come, that was certain. And as she gazed into the sky she became aware of her reflection in the dark window; she stared at it and through it to the empty waste, alternating between the two. She felt the familiar pull of all the emptiness and the silence that was her home claiming her once again.

Chapter Six

There was a scream over his head in the dark, and in the sudden silence that followed, his eyes darted at random tracing the shapes of objects in his room. The silhouettes the night had made of them took on menacing distortions, and as he stared, trying to distill them back into their true shapes—his chair, the books on his shelves—there was yet another scream, this time longer and louder: a fierce explosion in the darkness where he saw its bared teeth, the devouring smile…Snarling wild animals there…Then a door slamming hard and a fist coming down hard, pounding the door, and then another door slamming and then silence.

Wind shook the house. Another storm was coming. His parents were uptown at Nob's. It was Saturday. That's where they always went then. His heart was beating fast. All he wanted was to get back to sleep but he was wide awake now and it was no use.

He curled his legs and hugged his knees. He wanted to get up, but it was too hard to leave his pocket of warmth under the covers. All he could do was stare into the dark, letting the shapes there return once again to their original forms. The rope on the school flagpole across the street clanged away like a buoy at sea.

Christmas was coming so he thought about Christmas. They were practicing the second grade pageant now and he played Prince George.

"Here come I, Prince George; from Britain I have sprung. I'll fight the dragon bold, for my wonders have begun: I'll clip his wings, he shall not fly; I'll cut him down, or else I'll die."

He made his entrance through a trap door. It was fun to lie there listening for his cue from the King of Egypt above him: "Prince George, Prince George, walk in my son and heir! Walk in my son, Prince George, and boldly play thy part that all the people here may see thy wondrous art!"

The creaking floor, stray shafts of stage light cutting between the planks…

The other kids made fun of him and called him Prince George all the time now, but they were stupid and they stank like farmyards. Besides, he got to marry Sabra, who was Maggie Stolz, the prettiest girl in class, so they were just jealous as well as stupid.

It was nice to lie there and think about getting married to Maggie Stolz. They would live down in the woods out in the country behind the junkyard. That's where the old school marm used to live so they'd stay in her house. Yes. That would work out very nicely.

He didn't like school. The playground was the worst part. They had recess twice a day and he'd just stand back and watch everyone else. They'd play games and knock each other down then get up and knock each other down again. Afterwards, they'd swear and spit and talk about tractors. He'd watch them because he had to do something, but the worst part was he knew they were watching him too and every once in a while they'd come after him and chase him, screaming and swearing.

He looked around his room. In the darkness it was all still only a collection of outlines, a room full of shapes. Everything had a shape. Where did the shape come from? A square had four sides and all the sides were the same. A triangle had three sides. Every shape meant something. Junkers was shaped like a triangle. If you were flying in the air and you saw a triangle that would be Junkers.

His father had a plane once. Will said they used to fly all around the country in it, but they sold it a long time ago. There was a picture of the plane on the wall in the office—it's silver and it's standing in the middle of a stubble field. His father is sitting on one wing and Will is sitting on the other. The only thing left now was a propeller in the tin shed.

The tin shed was Grandpa Kern's old store. They moved across the street to the new one in 1958. Jim remembered that because that was the year he was born. The new store was made of brick with plate glass windows and a fake chimney. On the side of the chimney was a red and black International Harvester sign, an I inside of an H.

There were only pictures left now of Grandpa Kern's *very* first store – the one he had before the tin shed. It was made of wood and it took up most of mainstreet. Two tall skinny gas pumps stood out front, and the sidewalk was shaded by a canvas awning with "Kern's Hardware and Implement" printed on it. There was a wooden bench under the awning and off to the side was a glass door with a painted star where the post office was. There was an apartment up on the third floor where his parents lived when they first got married. Will liked to talk about the parties they used to have there. Everything was torn down now except for the back part where the shop was, but its walls were only crumbling yellow powder and a couple of years ago the roof blew off in a blizzard.

The tin shed heaved and groaned like a ghost ship. Even as he laid there in bed he could hear it, or at least know exactly the sound it made because it was always the same sound.

Nobody used the place anymore except to pile up old junk. Racks overhead were filled with rusty shafts and sickle bars. Hoses dangled from the rafters like black snakes. Slabs of iron and twisted metal were scattered all over the floor, and the floor was nothing but hard grease-packed dirt. Rows of radiators were lined up against the wall like tombstones nobody cared to claim.

And the propeller from the old plane, that was still there too, propped up in the corner against a pile of straw walkers covered in spider webs, and now in the winter the webs would be covered with frost. Rotting desks lined the office walls. Washed out papers and moldy forms stuck out from the pigeon holes. Shards of plaster lay everywhere. The glass in the window was shot out and the front door swung back and forth on a broken hinge. Snowdrifts piled up all winter; in the spring when the snow melted, birds flew in and made their nests; the summer rain soaked the floors and walls, then the rain turned to snow and the birds flew off and the drifts grew all over again. Walls made no difference. There was a metal sign nailed outside the office door: "Ecco."

A WD-9 tractor stood in the weeds beside the shed, sheltered by an ancient stand of oaks. The front tire cut into the ground at an angle, like a boxer Jim thought, with his foot dug in, ready to fight, just waiting for someone to come along. Will said they used to use the tractor for silage-making in the fall. Its flywheel ran a twenty foot belt hooked up to the silage wagon. That was when it took a couple dozen men to keep everything going. There used to be great big feeds at noon, and everyone just moved from farm to farm helping one another until all the work was done.

Next to the tin shed was the V.F.W. hall. It used to be called the Opera Hall and there were always traveling shows coming through, then after the war they tore out the stage, but they still used the building for smokers and bingo. There was a bowling alley in the basement, but it was closed down too. The walls were caving in now and it flooded every spring so water had sprung the polished wooden floors; every summer as the flood receded the curled boards were left like the ribs of some long extinct animal.

In the summertime, Jim liked to slip down the crumbling steps in back of the alley to escape the afternoon heat, and as his eyes adjusted to the dim light that crept through the glass blocks high up near the ceiling, the ruins around him would come to life. He knew only bits of town history that he managed to overhear, but the fragments played out in his mind and he pieced them together as best he could.

He knew that one night a young man and a young woman left the bowling alley together, and the next day some farmwife found her dead in his car out in the country. He strangled her with her scarf. One end was wrapped around her neck, and the other was tied to the steering wheel. Crime magazines came out and photographed it. Jim saw the pictures once when he was at Elmo Voivode's house. Elmo was the town cop.

"Lebensmude boy, got ten years. Not a boy anymore. Said it was an accident, that her scarf got caught in the steering wheel and it just kept getting tighter and tighter." Elmo trickled dry shreds of Prince Albert Tobacco into the trough of a cigarette paper, rolled the paper and licked the end. "Prettiest damn girl you ever seen. Blonde. No, black hair." He touched a match to the cigarette and blew out a lungfull of smoke. "He's back now, you know. Shoulda gassed the son of a bitch and be done with it."

Another storm was coming. The wind made it certain. The house shook like some beast rolling over in a winter lair…

Yes. It was the same thing, always. He was always lurking there…

He'd call out to him from the top of the stairs.

Come here. It's called "The Lost Half Hour."

Come here. It's called, "The False Knight Upon the Road."

"Oh where are you going?"

Said the false knight upon the road?

"I'm going to the school,"

Said the wee boy, and still he stood.

The animal stink, the metallic breath, his teeth gritting…

Come on, I'll give you fifty cents…It's all I've got…

It would be over soon.

He was always lurking there, and it would happen again and again. Fifty cents…

Sleep was impossible. A train was rolling by on the tracks south of town. The train used to stop three times a day for passengers. Morning, noon and night…It would be simple. He'd rehearsed it how many times? Just walk down there and wait in a gloomy yellow midnight depot, holding his ticket tight in his clenched fist, the telegraph key clicking, his bag sitting beside him on the wooden bench. Suddenly he would become aware of the floor beginning to vibrate, the sound of the train drawing closer, a whistle blast, the headlamp curving around the last bend south of town…

The pickup pulled into the driveway. The back door swung open and they both stumbled in laughing—his mother in a high piercing voice, his father in a low chuckle.

"But that's not what she said."

"Oh yeah it was," his father answered.

"I don't believe it."

"Don't have to."

She laughed again, and the more she laughed the more Jim felt his stomach tighten. He'd almost managed to get back to sleep, but now he knew it was no use. He kept muttering "shut up, shut up, shut up…" through clenched teeth as he pounded his pillow with his fist.

"It's cause they spend money like there's no tomorrow."

"Isn't that the truth."

"Yeah. Wha' d'ya say—little nightcap?"

Two glasses on the counter. The rattle of ice, the whiskey sloshing in…

They were quiet for awhile—they'd gone off to the living room. He couldn't make out anything they were saying—she giggled once in a while, but nothing else. He laid there, waiting. He knew the silence wouldn't last.

"I'm tired," she said. "I want to go to bed."

"How—just one more?"

"No."

"Oh come on…"

"No. And you've had enough too."

She went off to their bedroom. After awhile he followed her in.

Jim heard them through the wall—their room was right next to his. They talked some more, their voices low and unintelligible. Dresser drawers opening and closing. The covers drawn back. Another silence, and then suddenly she was struggling, screaming, "No! No..."

Jim's fists were still clenched as he muttered "Shut up!" Over and over into the darkness.

"No! No don't..." Her voice trailing off...

The bed shook. There was another silence.

She got up and inched down the hallway. Her hands guided her along the wall past Jim's room. The bathroom light flashed under his door, then it was dark again.

It's what always happened.

Jim stared wide-eyed into the dark, trying to make out the disjointed shapes hanging there. He listened to the sound of the snow grating against the windows. His mother was still crying, but not as much as before.

Chapter Seven

Jim dipped his fingers in the font outside the foyer; the icy water dripped down his wrist as a pious, deliberate sign of the cross took shape from his hand.

Oh come oh come Emma—a—an—uel,

Rejoice! Rejoice!

Oh I—I—Isra—el,

To thee shall come Emma—a—an uel!

A diaphonous curtain of incense waft dreamily through the air; he crept down the aisle to the pew his mother always took, the one behind Joe Bates and his wife. He performed a studied, balanced genuflection then knelt to the thinly padded board and said the Hail Mary, the Our Father, and the Twenty-Third Psalm. As he prayed he stared at the silver band of hair painted around the middle of Joe's skull.

It was Christmas day mass. He was alone because his mother, Lauerence, and Tip had gone to the midnight mass. He begged to go then, but his mother was adamant. It was too late for him. She told him to go to bed, but he didn't sleep—he laid there awake until they came home, then listened to them whispering and laughing in the kitchen. They each had a glass of Mogen David wine and they even put some Christmas music on the record player.

He sat back in the pew and stared at Joe's skull again.

Joe was the church janitor. Every morning you'd hear his Corvair stuttering to life, then he'd creep down the two empty blocks to the church to turn on the lights and to whisk out the pews with a straw broom. Winter mornings began even earlier because he let his car warm up over half an hour with a brick on the footfeed. Joe figured eightly miles an hour was as good a speed to idle as any, people joked politely.

Joe was also the janitor for the old school. Lauerence said once that everyone called him Master Bates, and then he laughed the way he did—all his teeth flashing. Jim didn't understand but he laughed anyway because they were with the von Leiche boys at the time and he didn't want to look stupid.

Joe's scalp was tight the way a mummy's skin would be. His smell was the smell of old men's skin, a sweat that was never washed out.

Jim wished he could have gone to the old school. Nuns taught there. He remembered watching them from his bedroom window gliding up and down the steps and working in the orchard, their black habits billowing in the breeze. They were called "crows," and it was funny to hear the name—he knew it wasn't a nice name, but they *did* look like crows.

The town tore out the orchard two years ago when they built the public school, and all the nuns moved to the Academy in Madrid. He felt cheated. He didn't like the public school—it was flat and made of bricks. There were only four classrooms and they all had brick walls and brick floors. The old school had three stories and a steeple; rooms were tucked away everywhere behind mysterious carved doors, long twisting hallways…

On the third floor there was a chapel. Outside there was a silver staircase that led up to it. At the top of the staircase you could see over the roofs of the entire town, and in the winter, when all the trees were bare, you could look out west and see the two black elevators where there used to be a town called Troy.

He knew there was another Troy from history, just like there was another Madrid from his maps. It was odd how two different places could have the same name. They weren't the same place. Or, they were and they weren't, because they *did* have the same name. A lot of people had the same name too. His name was Jimmy the same as Jimmy Pamocker. His middle name was George, but that was different because that was his Grandpa Sedler's name, just like Lauerence's name came from Grandpa Kern. You were always named after your family.

The old school was called St. Paul's, so it had the same name as the church, and that way it made sense.

It was fun to break into the old school. There was a window above the coal bin, and it was a simple operation to snake a piece of wire through the frame and unlatch the lock inside. To jimmy the lock.

He remembered last summer—how the crickets muffled away into silence as he crept through the hot, airless hallway. There was the smell of dust and books all around. The floors creaked; sunlight flooded the abandoned rooms, gold light pouring through massive dust-streaked windows.

He climbed the stairs and followed a maze of hallways through row after row of small rooms. The walls were covered with pictures of saints. Crucifixes hung everywhere. It's where the nuns slept, and just below their quarters was the library; everything there was bathed in a yellow and blue light that came streaming through the high mosaic windows. The tables and the chairs were carved with faces and twisted shapes. The shelves were black with the leathery spines of books. Dust floated through the slanting light.

God be with you.

And also with you.

He had been cheated.

The mass crept on.

Father Misere's voice was shrill and cracked as if his words were dragged over broken glass. A strange smile fixed itself upon his face like some impossible bird, yellow wings because of his teeth, nesting in the broad brown bole of his mouth. Then as he began the homily his face changed—the bird flew off, leaving only a cruel vacany, his gray eyes like two oily smears hurriedly painted on his ashen flesh.

"'Behold, a virgin shall be with child, and shall bring forth a son, and they shall call his name Emmanuel, which being interpretted is God with us.'"

He took a deep breath and steadied an oily gaze upon his tribe. "Though we are here to celebrate the season of our Lord's birth, we must also remember this child, the only begotten son of God, was born to die for our sins so that we may have ever-lasting life. And for those who doubt this, remember the words of Isaiah, prophysying the pain Christ would suffer, 'But he was wounded for our transgressions, he was bruised for our iniquities: the chastisment of our peace was upon him; and with his stripes we are healed.'

He paused, then repeated, "With his stripes we are healed," and let the sentence settle over the congreation until the last faint echo faded.

"Isaiah goes on to tell us that Christ was 'oppressed, and he was affflicted, yet he opened not his mouth: he is brought as a lamb to the slaughter, and as a sheep before his shearers is dumb, so he openeth not his mouth.'

"Where do we find this kind of selflessness, but in one whose origins are divine? This child of virgin birth who gave his life into the hands of the Jews, the disbelievers who crucified him for what they called the crime of blasphemy. If his teachings were blasphemous, then we are all blasphemers, and of course we are not. Yes, let us be like Christ, and in our oppression, let us open not our mouth. We are united in our faith in God's eternal love, a love so vast that he sacrificed his only son for us, for that is God with us."

Father Misere was the basketball coach too. Tip played basketball now. He started in the sixth grade—that's when all the boys had to try out. They lined up in the locker room with their pants pulled down, then Father Misere came by and squeezed their balls. If it hurt too much they'd be on the team.

Last year Jim's mother took him to a game. She screamed whenever Tip scored. Her long fingernails raked down her face.

He stared up at the stained glass windows; they were full of heavy blue and green colors like they were underwater. Angels were swimming through the sea. He started to get hot and dizzy.

"Take this and eat of it, for this is my body."

"Amen."

He got in line with the rest of them. It was his favorite part. He received his First Communion last spring. Afterwards he stood on the front steps of the church holding his new prayer book and rosary in its vinyl case with a little snap button on it. Jerry Hektner said, "Finally, won't be needing this any more!" Then he pretended to pitch his prayer book up at the sky. All the other kids laughed. Jim laughed too. Of course you couldn't throw it away, but it was funny the way he looked when he said it.

He crept closer and closer.

Body of Christ.

The salver floated under his chin. Father Misere's face hovered above. More skull than flesh. His fingers were like bundles of twigs raking out the translucent wafer from the shining gold ciborium.

Amen.

Father Misere set the host on Jim's tongue. The body of Christ was a taste in his mouth. It was blessed so it had a different taste now. Father said that would happen. One day in class he gave them all unblessed hosts to practice with. The sacred species. He wrote it on the board. Do not let it touch the teeth. Do not chew it. A mouthful of holiness. Only truth then.

He let it dissolve—it was big as a bolus. Medicine. Clay. Dry. Dust.

Dust....

His mother was grinding up a bowlful of hearts in the kitchen. There was the smell of onions frying in butter. All the windows were steamy from cooking.

Grandpa Sedler leaned straddle-legged against the radio at the far end of the living room. He peered into its gold face but was rewarded only with static as he turned the dial up and down the band.

"It doesn't work." Jim said.

His grandfather considered the dial a moment longer, then set his dentures rattling in soft stony accompaniment to his response. "Big fancy radio like this?"

"It needs a part."

"What kind of part?"

"I don't know. I just heard them talking."

"Smart cowboy like you ought to know how to fix it."

Jim blushed. Grandpa Sedler laughed like an engine trying to catch.

"Don't give him any ideas." Nora splayed a bundle of knives across the table at the other end of the room.

"Who's giving who ideas?" Grandma Sedler asked, entering with an armful of china.

"Oh, nothing. Just that old radio." The silver clattered into place, the plates following obediently behind. "Nobody has those anymore anyway."

"No I suppose not. Still…"

"It's old as the hills if you ask me."

"That's what Arly's for, isn't it? Get you a new one."

Nora threw her head back and laughed. "Not while there's another acre of land to buy somewhere."

Grandpa Sedler popped his teeth out of his mouth and nested them in his hand, examining them. "He's a gog foamer," He gummed.

"Daddy!" Grandma Sedler snapped. "How many times! Don't talk without your teeth."

"The—hur me."

"Get some new ones then. You just need them for eating, anyway."

"Tire—eating." He nodded in disgust.

Nora straightened the forks. "At least the record player works in it. Vivian gave me a boxful of all her old old opera records for Christmas."

"Opera!" Her mother laughed.

"Yes. Opera. I've been asking for them. She was getting rid of things for the move and I asked for them. I was going to pay but she wouldn't hear of it. she made it a Christmas present."

Grandma Sedler was still shaking her head. "I never heard of such a thing. What does Arly think?"

Nora adjusted a place setting in response.

"Where othe cow oys?"

"They're upstairs, daddy," Grandma Sedler said.

Smiling demurely to herself Nora headed out to the kitchen to check the meat.

Tip entered, tucking a single stray black hair neatly behind his ear. Lauerence followed after him a few paces, his own matted brown hair still uncombed.

"Look at that rat's nest." Nora chided with a wandlike wave of her spatula.

"Get him away from the mirror, maybe I could take care of it." He motioned gruffly with his head, pointing at his brother with the sharp blade of his chin.

Nora smiled. Grateful. Why? A commonplace. She ladled drippings over the turkey then slid it back in on the rack. It was Christmas.

"Let's rope 'em boys!" Grandpa Sedler called out, teeth firmly in place again. "Get this rodeo on the road! Got the three best cowboys in the territory right here! Rope 'em and take 'em down, what d'ya say!"

The three boys smiled at the illusory bulls that broke out of the coral everytime their grandfather greeted them.

The back door swung to with a frigid blast. Arly stomped the snow off his rubbers on the newspapers that laid spread out there beside the door, then shot a glance over the top of his glasses, the lenses white with frost. As he unbuckled his boots, swashing the snow left and right, he continued scanning, taking in the horizon until, satisfied with his findings, he kicked off his boots and ventured out of the porch and into the kitchen.

"What? Were you with the hogs?" Nora screwed up her nose.

"Yeah—it's—bad time..."

"Well go change already! I can't stand that smell, you know that! Your best clothes ..."

"Farm don't run itself," Arly mumbled on the way to the bathroom.

"Farm don't run itself," Nora mumbled in mimic response.

"Is that Arly?" Grandma Sedler sang out from the living room. "Is he back from church?"

"Yes," Nora said. "And he stinks to high heaven."

She jabbed the ham with a fork, watched the juices bubble out, then slid the meat back on the rack and let the oven door slam shut.

Grandpa Sedler stood at the living room window, suddenly chuckling with a low hoarse wheezing sound, his thick arms folded across his chest. He peered out across the snow, squinting as if taking sight of something far off in the distance.

"Dan Patch. Best horse I ever had. Ever tell you about the time I raced Hal Konig in his model T?" He was speaking to his grandsons but was still looking out the window, simultaneaously adressing the snow, his eyes still fixed on some invisible point.

"He just got this car and he was proud like a sow in heat—always out driving around in it, so one day I tell him a car's all right, but why bother when you got horses? So he bets me a silver dollar he can outrun me and old Dan in a race from my grainary to his, so that was two miles you see—and he says I can cut cross country and he'd still beat me, and I says no—no that wouldn't be fair, I'd race right along beside, and he just laughed and says it'd be the easiest dollar he ever made, and I thought to myself it'd be the easiest dollar I ever lost—'cause I know there ain't no horse can outrun a car, I know that, but what the heck I thought, it's worth a try. So we line up by my grainary there, that's the one—you know—my dad built—nineteen six with the first crop he took—still standin', so now what do you know about that?" He jabbed his finger in the air, interogating the snow, his story shifting now on a new tack. "That's something all right, that sure is something, and that house too out there, ain't no one lived there five years now—still there—so what do you know about that? Yes sir. You better believe it—my dad, he was a good man. He was a wise man. I ever show you the letters he sent me when he retired out to California? He knew things. That's what he did all right. Yes he did. He knew things. And my mother too. She was a good woman. Why she was a regular angel, she was. Don't tell me...Sure is something...Don't tell me...Yes it is..."

He peered even deper into the distance, then started off again, returning to his original course. "Lined up there we were, ready to go—so we take off —me and Dan in the ditch you see right beside the road and we're way out front from the start, but I glance back and see Hal and he's gainin' on me just like I figured, I hold him though—mile or more, oh yes, yes I did! Yes sir! Should of seen us—beautful, sleek brown, black mane—he could run all right—lightnin'! Yes sir, but then boom! There's Hal right up beside me and I can see him clear as day—grinnin' and laughin' like a monkey in a madhouse, but old Dan don't tell me he's not givin' a run, then Hal he finally pulls ahead—loses some when—slow down to make the corner—driveway, but I figure that's the end right there, then all of a sudden he stops dead—middle of the road! Old Dan and me just fly right by like the wind—just like that! Then I turn around and see Hal out screamin' and cursin' like a preacher on fire. And you know what happened? He run outa gas! Right there not a hundred yards from his grainary. Why I was laughin' so hard and he was cursin' so much his wife thought we was plumb out of our heads and so she comes walkin' down the driveway from outa the garden there, and then we finally settle down enough to tell her and she just shakes her head. Hal says to me, 'Well you won, fair and square,' and he give me the dollar. But I just give it back, 'better keep it' I says, 'looks like you could use it for gas!' Then you know what that old son of a bitch does? He don't buy no gas, I tell you that."

Peering into the snow, he lost himself in a private, conspiratorial snicker, then finally added, "He buys a bottle of whiskey then comes over and we sit out there by my granary, talkin' half the night. He was a good man. Been dead ten years now."

He glanced down at his grandsons, then his eyes returned to the snow one last time as if still waiting for something to appear, but the white waste revealed nothing other than its own self repeated over and over from one rising drift to the next. He let out a low chuckle…

Heads bowed in nervous piety…

Bless us—Lord
For these thy gifts
Which we—about to receive
Through—bounty of—flesh
Amen.

Arly sliced off a white slab of breast meat, his teeth clenched in concentration as he directed the knife along its steaming course then, letting the slice roll gently to the plate, he made another cut and another, praising the tenderness as he worked away at the shrinking brown carcass, its juices flowing profusely.

"C'mon! Eat!" He ejaculated.

Lauerence, sitting next to his father, took the plate, plucked up a drumstick, grinning as he made a clicking, sucking sound in the back of his mouth, then passed the platter to Tip.

"Save the neck for me." Grandma Sedler said. "Best part right there."

She took the plate from her husband, slipped the favorite portion to her own plate, then passed it on to her daughter. "So, what did Father Misere have to say about Christmas?"

Nora selected her turkey, set the platter in the middle of the table, then took the ham platter her mother offered. Her expression became thoughtful as she forked one of the red slices onto her plate. "He made some very good points, I think. Some very good points. Christmas isn't just a time…Well, it's a time to celebrate, but it's more—we have to remember why Christ was born, the sacrifice he made when the Jews crucified him."

Grandma Sedler forked off the tender strings of meat from the bony brown neck on her plate. "It's no wonder, is it? They *should* pay for that, after all." She twined the strands around her fork. "I don't like them, I know I shouldn't say that, but I don't."

Grandpa Sedler laughed. "Shouldn't say that! For all we know you're a Jew!"

"Daddy! Don't say such…"

"Well you got all that Bohemian blood in you, who knows what's in it?"

"There's no Jewish…"

"Jew, Indian, Chinesse, probably nigger blood too. Gypsy. Gypsy—that's what you are!" He laughed, punctuating the air with his knife as he spoke. "You know that, boys?" He turned to his grandsons. "You're Grandma there, she's a regular gypsy—now you got some of that in you, so you better be careful."

"Had—jeweler here, you know," Arly cut in. "Was a Jew. Scare your mother half to death."

"That's a fact too." Nora corroborated, remembering. "It was right after we got married—we were still living up in the apartment. One morning I took my watch over to him to fix. I don't know why, I should have just taken it to Madrid or Seneca. All I remember is he had these great big yellow teeth—like he was going to eat me. And then he invites me inside his house…I still have nightmares."

"What was his name, again?" Her mother asked.

"I don't remember any more."

"What was—now?" Arly asked the air in front of him, pausing between mouthfulls of stuffing to try and remember himself.

"He died though, didn't he?" Grandma Sedler asked.

"Died or moved away," Arly said. "Was—long time ago. Don't know why—ever come here in the first place."

"Neither do I." Nora agreed. "Good riddance. And the smell…" She waved her hand past her face.

"'Cause they don't wash. It's their religion," Arly explained. "Stink like niggers. Both from Africa, you know."

"And they can both go *back* to Africa," Nora said. "If you ask me."

The platters made the rounds once again.

"So," Grandma Sedler said, "We're going to have our first college boy here next year," Indicating Lauerence with the tip of her fork.

"Not—keeps monkeying up—way he does," Arly said.

"He'll do just fine, I'm sure."

"Well, least if he keeps away from—Indians," Arly responded, softening.

"What?" Grandma Sedler said.

"Don't remember? Last summer. Sisseton? He still got—scars. What happened again there—tell grandma."

Lauerence trapped a dripping brown forkfull of baked beans in his mouth, then scraping the fork clean against his teeth, he paused before swallowing, thoughtfully rolling them around on his tongue. "Well, you see," he finally started, "Last summer me and Whitey and Skeeter went down to a dance in Sissiton. After awhile it got so hot in the hall the three of us went outside for some air, and the next thing I know, these five drunk Indians are coming down the street and one of them picks a fight with me. All of a sudden all five of them are on me—I don't know why—and Whitey and Skeeter are trying to pull 'em off, We finally get out of there, but my hands are all cut up, my glasses are gone, my face is a mess."

"Shoulda seen him," His father shook his head.

"I remember now," Grandma Sedler said. "Didn't you ever catch 'em?"

Lauerence shrugged. "I didn't know who they were."

"And South Dakota too," Arly added. "Just decided—let it go."

Lauerence nodded and made a clicking sound in his mouth.

His story was a lie, but it passed muster once again. The truth was that Whitey and Skeeter took off without him for a prank and he was so drunk he jumped on back of the car and hung on until Whitey started fishtailing. Lauerence flew through the air at twenty miles an hour until he ground his hands into the gravel and came to a bloody stop in the gutter. There *were* five Indians, but they were standing on the sidewalk laughing at him, then they just walked away.

He wore his Indian fable proudly now as well as the fiction of his wounds, stigmata whose private value changed with his mood. The only others who knew the truth were Tip and Jim, but they were sworn to secrecy. At first he cursed himself, ashamed, feeling guilty of the lie, but soon realized he too could easily believe his own fabrication and let it slowly eat away and replace reality and truth. His father upheld the story immediately. It confirmed everything he knew. Indians were trouble.

Grandma Sedler balanced the gravy boat in one hand, ladling out brown dollops with the silver spoon in the other. "And you're going to be a writer." She said proudly.

"Yeah, that's what I want to do."

Grandpa Sedler jabbed at the air with his fork. "Got the whole history of the place right here—right here! That's what it is, that's what it is all right! Just like my Dad—he was a writer too—sure he was. He wrote me letters you know, out from California. My dad was a very wise man and that's what it takes. You kids never knew him—but that's what he was—a wise man. Your dad knew him though, and his dad knew him too. Isn't that right, Arly?"

Arly tipped his own fork in mute acknowledgment before impaling another slice of ham on its prongs; continuing his assent with a parsimonious nod, he lifted the red meat over to his plate.

"Brothers! That's what they were! Your Grandpa Kern and my Dad—and Grandpa Kern and me, we're like brothers too. You know that's how your mother and father met—it was because your Grandpa Kern wanted to teach Arly and Bill how to farm, and my dad could out-produce *any* farmer in Ashkenaz County—whole of North Dakota for that matter—yes he could! Don't tell me he couldn't! So Lauerence, he hired these two here out to my Dad in the summer. And there's your mother out there too." He poked Tip in the ribs and rattled his dentures. "Course she was the prettiest girl around! Had men lined up all over the state!"

"Oh Daddy!" Grandma Sedler said, Nora laughing beside her, white teeth flashing, a coy hand waving across her face.

"Was a good man," Arly mumbled, temporaily lodging a mouthful of ham in his cheek to make room for the clear operation of his tongue. Moving the meat back into place he swallowed hard and washed it down, draining another glass of Mogen David. He re-filled it from the bottle on the shelf behind him.

Grandpa Sedler looked down at his fork; his eyes followed it as he set it aside. He drank off his own glass. "Yes he was."

Jim put his silverware down. He folded his hands.

"You done?" His father asked.

"Yes."

"Got a nickle's worth of ham left on your plate."

"I can't eat it."

"Shouldn't—taken it then."

"I'll eat it!" Tip offered, forking it away, giving his brother a playful nudge.

"He's just got his eyes on the dessert," Grandma Sedler said.

"Well if he wants desert he's going to have to go down in the basement and get the ice cream," Nora said.

The wooden stairs cut steeply down to the gray cement floor; dim shadows grew out of greasy-brown bulbs dangling between cobweb rafters. The steps were built into the side of the cistern near the top of which an opening was hewed out, a crude portal filled with shimmering blackness. The cistern was cracked, its walls broken so it couldn't even *hold* water any more, but they still used it. A dank black pool, it would pull you in, it would take you…

The freezer stood next to the fuel oil tank, both wedged in a greasy alley beside the furnace, an oily monolith, countless spidery legs hooked to the ceiling, vents lost in the webs where still more spiders lived. When it kicked in you could feel it rumbling through the floor and walls clear up to the attic, wheezing out through the black registers a few precious inches of heat. It did little to displace the cold which remained intact even on the sunniest days, still it was comforting to huddle against the register in the corner of his room wrapped in a blanket to trap the stray whisps of warmth, listening to the motor droning away muffled far below.

He poked through the frozen meat until he found the ice cream.

"Hog market gone up. See that George?"

"I think you were right to buy in when you did."

"I know I was right."

Arly had already left the table when Jim returned. He was sitting in his chair, the latest Dakota Farmer in his lap. He was quiet now except for occasional appreciative grunts concerning the health of the market.

Grandma Sedler heaped a pile of bones and fat onto a plate in the kitchen. "Lauerence might just become as famous as anyone, who knows?"

Her daughter laughed and slid a handful of knives into the brown soapy water.

"After all, Zdenka Trinka is a shirt tail relative, and she's a writer. I never read her books, but that's one."

A Little Village Called Liddice. Around somewhere. Zdenka Trinka. Treblinka. Penciled houses on the cover. What was it about anyway? Who knows…

"And another, Ida Prokoff Lee. That would be Laurence's great aunt."

Yes. Now that was something. Her sculptures on the capital grounds. Pictures, a thousand dollars apiece…

Upstairs, Laurence pawed through an inky journal. His teeth set, he tapped his ball point against the desk until he came to the page where his looping webs of feverish script left off, then he attacked another entry.

"Bastards and hypocrites! Sure. Why not call it that? My first book. I'll tell all about this place. Call *me* Stooge. *They're* the damn stooges. Curly, Moe and Larry—what they don't know is Larry's a *smart* one. I'm smarter than all of them put together. I could kill them with a single thought. That's what I'm going to do too! And Dad thinks I'm going to flunk out. I'll show him! He thinks I'm going to flunk out and come back to take over the store. I'll show him! I'm going to get so far away from this place…I'm going to show the whole world!"

He looked over what he'd written. It was rambling and pointless, but he didn't care. He was angry and it felt better just to write *something* down as he remembered for the thousandth time what happened in Sisseton and the countless other indignities he suffered at the hands of his family and his classmates. "C'mon Stooge! Can't you catch us!" Skeeter's words echoed hatefully. Why did he run? They goaded him and he ran. He did exactly what they wanted him to. What did it get him? He rubbed the scars on his palms.

"I'll leave *them* in the dust. Damn fools. Going straight into the army. Stupid. 'They pay you good, just go kill the gooks—that's what they call 'em you know. Shootin' gooks. Come home on leave. Think all the girls you can get!' And then the way he laughed when he said it. Bang, Skeeter, your dead. I"m the one that'll get the girls. I'll just rip their clothes off and take them!"

A wave of lust washed over him. He looked back at his last sentence. "Yes. I'll be all over their tits. Great big tits…"

He threw himself back on his bed.

Grandpa Sedler gave his belly a slap and winked at Tip. "Iron! What d'ya think? Gonna have a whole herd—you three boys. Gonna call it the Big K Ranch. No…*Circle* K. That's it. Teach you how to raise 'em and breed 'em. That's what I'm gonna give each of you boys. Gonna be horse traders, just like your Grandpa! Gonna split everything up three ways!"

"I don't know Grandpa. Do you really think…"

"Hell, boy! What else is there? Herd of Apaloosas! Nothin' pretttier. That's a fact!"

Arly grunted in his sleep.

Grandpa Sedler filled his wine glass, drank it off, then quickly refilled it. He took his usual stance at the window—legs planted wide, arms folded across his chest. As the wine took effect he lost himself in Apaloosa dreams.

Nora and her mother were working in the cellar—some of the potatos were going bad so they had to sort them again. Their voices rose muffled through the floorboards, but everyone else in the house was quiet—each drawn into his own accustomed solitude, and so the holiday wore on; then, near twilight, Arly stirred himself awake. It was time to do the chores.

"Go get your brothers." He called out to Tip studying at his mother's desk in the back of the room. Obediently and wordlessly Tip followed the order.

Soon all three brothers were getting into their work clothes in the porch, pulling up their jeans stiff with dirt and patches of manure, tucking in the tails of their torn and mended shirts.

They crowded into the pickup, breath hanging white in the air while Arly went through the ritual combinations of choke and throttle to coax the engine to life. When it finally caught they had to wait another five minutes for it to warm up, otherwise it would kill.

A handful of ravens lifted into the sky. A great white plume of exhaust enveloped the idling truck. The heater roared away with an icy blast. No one spoke.

Behind them, the sun was sinking into its own red blood as Arly navigated the half mile road to the farm through a portal in the frosted window the size of quarter.

Jim slid back the gate behind one of the sow's stalls in the finishing barn and scraped the cement slats clean with a hand hoe. He closed the gate, then, bracing a trap door in the floor open against his knee, he dropped the manure into the honey pit. Sometimes a sow laid on one of its little pigs and smothered it, so Jim would have to pick the flattened corpse out of the shit and burn it in the trash barrel next to the grove. There were almost two dozen stalls in the barn and he had to clean each one.

The sows frightened him, but he liked the little pigs. He felt bad for them when they died and he also felt bad for them when they got their shots and their teeth cut. He'd cradle the little pink squirming creature in his arms while his father snipped each of its teeth with a side cutter, then sprayed its nuts with Lysol and, after an expert slice with a razor blade, squeezed the balls out between his fingers, cut them loose, then let them drop to the cement—a soft plop of jelly brown and red joining the others at their feet. Finished, Jim set the pig back in its pen. Castrated and toothless, it hobbled away to the plywood under the heat lamp and collapsed, its legs flinching.

Arly was feeding hay to the cows. High up on the stack, he dropped the green alfalfa bales down into the feeder that rimmed the stack, then climbed down to slip the twines off. He scattered the fresh green slabs around the feeder. Some of the cows were already coming up to eat. They poked their curly brown and white heads between the boards, their breath rising white in the cold, and with slow passive licks of their broad tongues scooped out leisurely mouthfulls of the fresh summer-smelling hay.

Laurence was feeding silage. The cart was suspended on an iron rail above the feed bunks; he nudged it along with one hand and, with a long curved fork in the other, distributed the sweet-smelling feed into the wooden bunks. Slowly the cows filed out of the barn, their tails swishing, summoned by the familiar sound of the cart rolling along the bunkline. Broad red tongues licked away at the rich, pungent corn.

Inside the barn, Tip was spreading straw. The loft was filled to the rafters with golden bales, a dozen of which he'd already tossed to the ground. He scrambled down the ladder, opened the bales with athletic flourish, then twirling the twines in the air, he lasooed them over a fence post and went to work, vigorously kicking the loosened straw into an ever widening radius until the entire barn floor was covered with a soft rich carpet ready again for the cows to bed down in for the night.

It was completely dark by the time everyone finished. A few yard lights flickered, but the only other light came from a pale half moon and the thick net of stars cast around it.

Cold and wordless, they shivered themselves back into the pickup and headed home.

Grandma And Grandpa Sedler were gone now. Nora sat at her vanity. "Now everyone smells to high heaven! Get cleaned up. Hurry! We're going to be late."

It was customary to spend Christmas evening at Grandma and Grandpa Kerns. There was always a huge meal and nearly a couple dozen realtives and friends, so Nora was carefully selecting her outfit, after all, the Neidhammels would be there from Madrid and the Verderbs from Seneca would also be there.

Smoke and laughter filled the room.

Ken Rarly smoothed a black streak of hair into its proper groove over the top of a greasy silver skull as he studied himself in the mirror behind the candy dishes. Arly was standing beside him. He scooped up a handful of honeyed nuts and tossed them into his mouth, then washed them down with his whiskey seven.

"Santa Claus been good to you, Arly?" Ken took another exacting measurment of the space between the shiny locks.

"Suppose."

Satisfied with his coiffed precision, he spoke now to Arly's reflection. "You're a good man. Lot of people depend on you. Just like your Dad. You know exactly what I'm talking about too." Ken gave the glass a quick nod accompanied by strange equivocating laughter. He emptied his drink, slid off the edge of the mirror, then disappeared down the hallway.

Upstairs, Jim listened to all the muffled voices from below as he wandered through a maze of half a dozen rooms. It was the house his father grew up in. His room had been the small one that looked out over Maple's Grove. Next was the maid's room when they had a maid, and after that, next to the toilet, was the big room where Grandpa Kern's first wife died.

She had influenza. She caught it right after they got married. It took her only two days to die. Her last name was Schonheit. They had a daughter named Mary, but she moved to Scotland thirty years ago. The room was used for storage now—steamer trunks stuffed with clothes and shoes, wooden crates nailed shut, furniture piled up everywhere, all of it stained a heavy black. The walls were covered with pictures; Jim studied them in the half light.

Bland, unsmiling faces stared back at him through the mist of forgotten time. Nameless and dutifully posed against impossible backgrounds, they looked out with gray eyes in mute sadness: all their fictions had been betrayed.

His great grandfather Louis Kern sat behind the wheel of a long, shiney black automobile, and next to him sat Minnie, his wife, wearing an enormous white bonnet that looked like a pillow strapped to her head. They emigrated from Prussia in 1864. He was an officer in the Prussian army and he played the violin, in fact he was one of the king's favorite musicians; then one day he killed another soldier in a duel. The penalty was execution, but since the king liked him he gave Louis a choice: execution or exile. So Louis ended up in Junkers.

His face, nearly inscrutable behind great walrus whiskers, was the only shadowy link now to that far away world. The story Will had told him—Jim remembered the first time he heard it, how it transported him instantly to a fairy tale land with soldiers, musicians, kings, duels—was impossible to believe, especially against the other photos on the wall. The ashen expression on his grandfather's face, his eyes cast down, his head crooked to the side, betrayed no connection to his own father's steady, piercing eyes looking level into the lense, and the dignity of that gaze was completely erased in the next photo—that of Jim's own father whose prematurely balding head wore its feeble disguise of painted black hair in an attempted arrest by his vanity. His spectacled eyes were of another species altogether whose past had been deliberately erased and whose amnesiac glare betrayed only the erasure and nothing else. Eyes of bland imprecation—the same as in Jim's dream of his father: him brandishing wickedly a loveless Abraham blade, then with drunken, unconscious flourishes slicing through the air, flinging drops of blood with every pass.

Snow grated against the glass. They were all dowstairs. John Woiwode, Charlie Krause, Carl Witt, John Wendt, Jim Webster...He listened to their voices as he stared through the window. They were all voices from the store—Grandpa Kern's cronnies. That's what Grandma Kern called them, then she laughed. Grandpa Kern would be sitting on the sofa. He probably hadn't said a thing all night. He just sat there in his white shirt and bow tie. He was smoking a cigarette; his black pants were covered with ash and his head was crooked to the side. Years ago he got stuck in a blizard out in the country and spent the night in his truck. Since then his neck was always frozen that way. If you touched it, it would be cold in that spot.

Last summer Jim was in the office working his broom around his grandfather's shoes, sweeping up the ashes there, careful not to disturb him. But suddenly the old man roused himself out of the chair, went over to the till then pulled a five dollar bill from the drawer.

"Here," he breathed, handing Jim the money. "Run over—have Charlie give—carton—cigarettes."

Grandpa Kern always chose one of Jim's brothers for errands, so even though rain was pouring out of the sky and all the streets were flooded he was excited for the responsibility suddenly bestowed upon him. He paused a moment at the door before running off. Colorless liquid upon colorless glass.

He raced across the crumbling sidewalks, streaming brown rivulets running into the river of mainstreet, then scurried past the steps of the abandoned hotel, its creaking yellow sign swinging idiotically in the wind. Garbage scudded through the street and some paper tangled around his legs so he had to reach down and tear it away. He was completely soaked now—the only other people who were outside were working by the butcher shop, hauling a hog carcass out of a pickup box.

In ashen revery Charlie Gaughn stood at the cash register staring out into the rain as if expecting some vague miracle. Jim handed him the soaked bill.

Charlie's skeleton hand reached up to the shelf behind him and extracted a carton of Old Golds.

"Gonna turn to snuff by the time you get back." He warned.

Grandpa Kern took the carton from Jim's dripping hands. When Jim offfered up the fistfull of change—a dollar and two quarters—his grandfather took it, then pointed to the quarters in his palm. "You take those. Don't tell your dad though."

His gray fingers dropped the coins in midair…

Chapter Eight

Fifty cents swimming in his brother's hand, his cold basement touch, the promise not to tell…

His words dropping their poison into his ear…

Jim washed himself in the bathroom. He was still trembling.

He hid the fifty cents in his desk, then sat there in his chair staring out the open window. Hot wind rippled through the curtains. He traced his finger through the dust on the sill.

The pigs were feeding on the Waisenhaus farm just north of the school playground. They poked the lids on the feeders open with their snouts, then when they finished the lids slammed shut again with a tin slap that left a dull gray echo against the buildings.

The Old Home bread truck rumbled by. Rust yellow with a rusting red stripe.

His mother was listening to her opera records in the living room.

It was always the same…

"Listen, you don't understand. I got to do it…

"You wrote this story? Eight years old? I'm about as jealous as jealous can be. This is really very good."

He looked at it and said that it was good. The flush of pride meant everything. To put words on the page…

"Listen, you don't understand. I got to do it. Fifty cents. it's all I have. Take it…Your story is so good…"

He looked down at the story on his desk. The words were dead now. It was all dead. He was alive and then he was dead.

It was that simple.

But Lauerence would be going away to college in two months, and that would be the end of it. He would have to leave him alone then. It was best when he was alone. He knew all the best places to hide too: in the church, in the old school, in the grove behind the school, in Maples grove where the old well was—there were plum trees there and they'd be getting ripe soon, he remembered now as he went through the list. He had to keep finding new places though, otherwise his mother would find him. Wherever he went her eyes spied him out. And he could never stay away long—that was the rule. Every hour he was supposed to come back home and check in. Then sometimes Lauerence would be there, like he was today…

One night last spring he was carrying around all the change Laurence had given him over the last few months—a heavy silver pocketful, and from out of nowhere she suddenly appeared and started to undo his belt, explaining. "I'm doing the wash now—Everything you're wearing…" Then her hand brushed the heavy bulge, and what had passed for a smile on her face changed instantly to alarm as her fingers surrounded the cylindrical shape she had discovered. She pushed him down and tore the pants off his legs, spilling the money all over the floor.

"Where did you get this! Where did you get all this!? Answer me!"

"I got it from the store." The truth was impossible.

"Just what I thought! You little thief. You're nothing but a little thief! You know where little thieves go? They go straight to hell! Do you want to go to hell? That's exactly where you're going! Wait until I tell your father—you think you're in trouble now, just wait until he finds out. Flunking all your grades and now this—a rotten little thief!"

She had scooped up a handful of quarters, and now she flung them at him and slapped him hard as stood, naked, trembling.

She gathered up the clothes and left, slamming the door to his bedroom behind her. He had lied and she believed the lie. It was easier to lie. And so he would lie. And Lauerence would be gone soon.

He crawled under the covers afterwards. One electric shock after another coursed through his body. The lie had become the truth. So the truth could be only a lie.

So he started stealing then to satisfy the lie. What did it matter? His fingers slipped easily into the till, he found. It suited him.

"Go to work everyday—put—roof over your head!"

"And he steals it! He's just a little thief…"

He sat there listening to the music and the wind. His back was still sticky against his shirt. He tried to rub it dry against his chair…

The breath, hot, metallic; his skin cold and sweaty like basement walls. The green chalkboard there. A, B, C…He held the chalk in Jim's hand, tracing out the letters. Lauerence taught him how to write and how to read before he even started school. That's how it all started.

It didn't matter though. They were thinking about sending him away—he didn't talk—that's what they told him. They had some other words for it too, but they just kept telling him that he had to talk and he had to mix in. But everyone else stank and they were stupid and they said stupid things. He wanted to be alone. It was best that way…

Beloved spouse, and dost thou leave me now?

By sad lament I'm torn,

Nora followed the libretto at her desk. She had lowered all the shades: a globe of green light glowed dimly across her scattered books. Finally the house was quiet. It was good to forget about everything and concentrate on the music. It drove everything else way.

My senses are oppress'd by grief,

And thou, so cruelly, canst give

No help to me!

O Gods! O stars!

It's my own secret. He's a monster who lives at the top of the stairs.

And must I then prepare
Once more to die?
Without thy dear embrace,
With no goodbye?

She closed the libretto and swooned, sinking back in her chair, the music washing over her. *She* had found a way...It's my own secret...Could she be as sweetly condemned?

God looked back at her...It was good to be punished by God...

Jim stood in the kitchen, drinking a glass of water.

"What are you doing? Come here."

Jim obeyed and entered the living room.

"What are you doing?"

Jim shrugged his shoulders in response. She was just a shadow in the back of the room.

"You stick around here now. I might need you for something later."

It was too hot to go outside anyway, Jim thought, resignedly. For some reason, he didn't move.

"Well, what are you going to do?"

He shrugged again then wandered off.

She worried about him. It was humiliating to realize he was retarded, but the more she thought about it over the last year since Mrs. Melpo told her, the more resigned she became. He could do *something.* He wasn't an idiot. He was just slow. It was a burden and she needed to find an answer. It was part of the punishment. When one lived, one was punished, purified. I will be pure before my God. The world is an orphanage and heaven is my home.

They may not need to send him away. If he could just get by. Mrs. Melpo said it might be possible—he would never be like Tip...Of course he didn't have to be. College was out of the question—Mrs. Melpo had explained that too. Nora agreed. It was odd to think about college for someone going into the third grade, but she agreed with Mrs. Melpo—it was best to be prepared for all this ahead of time—it would be easier if she didn't expect too much out of him so she wouldn't be disappointed later on. It was becoming easier already. It was impossible not to be disappointed though—but as long as she had Tip—and even though Lauerence was the wild one, Sister Ludlam *did* say he was one of the most intelligent students she ever had. "He was my special pet, you know," she confided to Nora graduation night, "You might have some kind of a genius there," at the same time warning Nora never to let him know it. Nora agreed only too readily—he already had a big enough head, the last thing he needed was someone telling him he might be a genius. She would keep her pride in a private stock. Maybe he could be a writer after all—famous. They always had difficult lives—she'd been reading about them and it helped her accept his tantrums—last week even, running out of the house at supper time in his bare feet, screaming like a madman…

Lauerence sprawled across his bed, beads of sweat on his brow and bare chest, then he sat up, put on his underwear and ran his hands through his shaggy brown hair over and over. The windows in the gable were jammed open as far as possible, but not even the slightest breeze stirred the heavy air. Flies were buzzing at the screen. From downstairs he recognized familiar muffled strains. *Orfeo ed Euridice.* The blood red cover propped against her desk.

He rubbed his finger tips together, letting his hair draggle over his face. Almost. Almost there. What I think…What I'm going to do…Focus…He ran off…The goddamned track. He ran off the track. He ran off the damn track. Everything you're supposed to do. He's not going to do it. He's not going to stay on track. He's going to be a runner. He's going to win races. Then after awhile he can't stay on track anymore. He can't run the same race. It could start as a story. Well, it would be a story at first. It would be a story. His own rules. His own kind of race.

His fingers took up the straggling tips of his hair, and as his sat, completely immersed in his own thoughts, he unconsciously stroked and rubbed again and again what became a wringing-wet mop.

Suppertime.

Arly ran some water in the sink, then made a few haphazard swabs of the washcloth over his blackened fingers. He eyed himself in the mirror as if he didn't know what he expected to find. He wiped his hands dry.

He was the last to the table as Nora, impatiently attending the meal, began to pass around the platter full of corn on the cob. Tangled wisps of her hair fell across her face, painting fine black lines in the stark white. He slid three cobs to his plate, then suddenly cocked his head aside, scraped his chair back across the linoleum, jumped off to the living room and turned up the television news. "Weather's almost..." he explained as he reseated himself. He sliced off thick slabs of butter and ran them up and down each cob with his knife.

Lauerence's square steel jaws sliced away at the wide yellow rows; beside him, Tip had just finished one cob—he dropped it into the pile in the middle of the table, then with the same dexterous move slid another one onto his plate; Jim was working away at his own cob, rolling it back and forth across a pool of melted butter.

Lauerence looked up, wiping at a greasy spot on his face.

"Dad, I..."

"Quiet! Weather's on!" Hunched, Arly glared over the top of his glasses, face to the plate, wrists firmly planted against the table edge. Lauerence shrugged and grabbed another cob.

Dewy Berquist's voice on the television explained what to expect for tomorrow. Arly listened, a mouth full of unchewed corn, intent on each syllable.

Nora managed to eat half a cob, but no more.

Gluck. Gloook. Glooooook. She pronounced inside her head. It has a happy ending. That's what's nice about it...He gives it a happy ending—after all it's not *supposed* to end that way—he looks back and *that's* the end. But he changes it.

Her hand went up to wipe a bead of sweat from her brow.

"Get—barley out. Good!" With the back of his fingers Arly swiped the grease from his mouth. Stray corn kernels that clung to the black whiskers on his chin fell off to the floor. The jingle man sang the Old Home song.

"Can we talk again?" Nora said.

"What? Don't gotta be that way!" Arly slid back from his plateful of riddled cobs. "That's what I live by—forecast!"

"I know what you live by."

He spit in the sink. "What's that supposed—mean?"

"Just what it sounds like."

"Oh be quiet already!"

After supper the three boys went out to the backyard and tossed the cobs over the lilac bushes. They fell one by one through a quivering web of flies stretched across the rotting piles of garbage on the grove floor. The flies rose and flung themselves back in rhythm with the falling cobs, then finally the web stitched itself back together again in one complete mass of undulating blackness as the boys stood watching mutely, in the still night mosquitoes blanketing their bare arms and faces, streaks of blood there mixed with sweat.

A car rolled to a stop out front. It was Mat Steiner—one of Tip's friends. Matt's father was driving them to the movie in Madrid. Tip took off while Lauerence and Jim stood watching the car drive away, then Lauerence headed for the house, glancing furtively over his shoulder at Jim as he walked.

Jim listened again to the flies, then looked down at the mosquitoes on his arms, amazed by their tiny bodies—how they bloated up with his blood then flew away. The slightest breeze began to rustle through the grove.

The screen door slapped back on its hinges and his father shot out of the house then headed down the walk to the pick-up. Jim positioned himself behind the dead oak at the end of the driveway and watched.

Arly moved in quick short steps, eyes cast groundward; he raked a blackened hand through the black hair streaked across his balding skull. He pulled his hat down tight, but just before climbing into the truck, he cocked the hat back, snapping the brim with a suddenly jaunty flair.

It was pleasant kneeling next to the tree. The bark peeled away, charred black from a lightning strike, and animals made nests in all the hollows. A red-winged blackbird sang out its clear bell-like notes.

Arly backed away and drove off…

"Whiskey-Seven?"

"Double."

"Hot one."

"Yeah."

"Barley in?"

"Tomorrow."

"Yeah? Seven to one she rains."

"Forecast—good. Keep—change."

"Hear about Harv?"

"Yeah."

"Lucky he wasn't goin' any faster. Couldn't even walk when he left last night—I saw that. Drives right in the ditch just like he's pullin' into his own garage. It's pretty funny when you think about it."

"He—quite a guy."

"Damn lucky."

"That's—fact."

Arly spit, knocked back his first drink, ordered another and waited.

Mother keeps screwin' up—books. Couldn't believe…Stay your own damn business. Gettin' so damn old—can't even add. Just wanta say—get the hell out my store…

Anna Lee slapped her coin purse down on the bar tap and swung her long bare legs around the stool. "Looks like *someone's* lost in thought here! What'cha doin? Solvin' all the problems in the world?"

"Nah. Jus'…"

"Don't tell me. I know what you're up to. It's my job as a member of the mayor's cabinet to read his mind. Let's see now. Farmers givin' you a hard time, everybody wants credit, and you're worried about the crops."

"You're pretty good."

"Maybe I'll get a crystal ball and go into business." She laughed. "Yeah. Why not? Be just like those gypsies that used to come through here, camp outside of town."

Arly laughed.

"The way your dad used to go after 'em…"

"Well, they're worse than Indians. And dirty…" He waved his hand past his face in disgust.

"What do you think happened to 'em all?"

He shrugged.

"I imagine they're all dead by now," Anna Lee said.

"Oh yeah. That was back—Depression. Dead or jail, suppose."

"Well, if I can't be a gypsy then, I'll just settle for an ordinary barfly. "Nebo! What's a girl gotta do to get a drink around here?"

"Whatever comes natural." Neb rubbed at a dirty spot on a glass, then filled it with Catawba.

"I'll tellya what comes natural—dancin' up a storm! That's me! You know that though—I'm an open book!"

Neb scraped her money off the bar top, re-filled Arly's drink and headed off to the register. "A man in my position has to know everything. I'm right up there with all the chief gods—bartenders and grave-diggers —*those* are the oldest professions—don't let anyone tell you different."

Anna Lee Drank her wine in long swallows. "So, Arly, how's your dad?"

"Don't do much."

"No. Suppose not. How's his health?"

"Pretty good. He don't complain."

"Thought he went to the doctor."

"Just—check-up."

"Everything's still tickin', huh?"

"Yeah. Tell ya—what's drivin' me—up—wall, it's mother."

"Oh oh."

"Keeps screwin' up the books. Then she won't mind her own business either."

"Well, you're gonna have to fire her then."

"I want to, believe me." He emptied his drink and spit. "Family...And then, I go back in the shop—check on mechanics—and what do you think they're doin'? Standing around talkin' all the time! Don't know how many times I tell 'em—shut up and get to work already!"

"Well fire them too!"

"I'm thinkin' about it—especially Dell. But that's family again—Shirttail."

"Dell?"

"Yeah. His mother was—sister to my dad's first wife. *I'm* not related to him, but what—gonna do? Just talks and talks..."

"That'd drive me crazy too, I guess." She finished her wine. "Too much talk spoils the fun."

It was hot in the car. The mosquitoes were bad, so they kept the windows rolled. The neon "Nebo's, Nebo's..." flashed its red reflection on the glass.

Nora sat at her desk in the darkened room.

Let no man ever doubt my pow'r!
You loving pair so venturesome,
Return unto the world above!
A thousand trials are repaid
By a requited love!

A cool evening breeze rustled through the curtains. She decided to listen to the entire opera one more time.

Chapter Nine

The stroke left his vocal cords paralyzed, but Dr. Schadow told Arly the condition might be only temporary; nonetheless, the best place for his father now would be the nursing home in Seneca. It was a good home, and the family could visit whenever they wanted. Arly consented, his mother agreed, arrangements were made.

A lump of gray cinder shoveled into a wheel-chair, he glared into the distance—the parched brown lawn out his window sloping down to a dry creek bed—his mind struggling with the fragments of memory left to it as if piecing together a shattered mirror: no matter how closely the shards were made to fit, the surface would never again be smooth, but only a puzzle of refractions and distortions. The gnarled stump of his hand made its way to his mouth, there to wipe the spittle from his lips, then returning to his lap, his fingers picked at the coverlet over his knees.

He listened to his voice inside his head, only the words made no sense to him. He had always been here, in this room. The view out the window had always been the same…A picture of him—it had to be him—sitting at a table beneath an enormous tree—the redwoods. A bottle raised he salutes the camera…Obscure memories kept safe somewhere, projections in a dark chamber, but all turned around…He had always been here. Had to keep an eye on himself. Tired. A man gets worn out. He just gets worn out. Needs to rest.

George had been by earlier, but Lauerence remembered only vague traces of the visit—what little there was to remember. He stood at the window looking out at the same dry creek bed: "You'll be out, no time. Know what I done? Bought me a ranch—Triple K—for the boys—that way—always have a place—come to…That's—story of George Sedler—that's what I do—that's what I always done—you know that—just like the old days—remember? Just like you—built this land—yes sir—the Triple K, that's right—then traded the Ford for three quarter ton. Lotta hay to haul. Yeah. You'll be out, no time."

Repeated in random order the litany of essential facts and dreams returned to Lauerence who, in drugged and mute oblivion, cradled his too-heavy head dodderingly in his hand, his yolk-colored eyes staring into the brown dead land; words faded in and out, re-arranged themselves. Legends were for the living.

He slept, leaving all such things as legends are made of to George alone, whose only real possession was the belief in his own past—more so as that past became further and further separated from historical fact, and took on with equal zeal both the ornament of supremely heroic, absolutely fictitious deeds and the luxury of the deliberate repression of all the lies and all the wasted years that were also too much a part of their lives. Even though they were remolded with each retelling and reimagining, the stories would still follow familiar contours of myth and forgetting. George was better at it anyway…

Their German-speaking fathers met in the mills in Minneapolis then came out here—well they used ox-carts—his dad you know got quite a bit of trouble—killed a man in a duel—that's a fact—you can look that one up if you want—it's all right there, sure it is—so he had—come over—from Prussia you know—why, the place he come from, not even there anymore—no sir—try lookin' for it—won't find it—guarantee it! Yes sir, what do you know about that now? So they come out here then—farmers, homestead—outside Utopia, —that's no place to be found now either—just graveyard there, maybe not even that anymore—used—sell horse there—well—sold horses all around here. Then Lauerence and me we grew up like brothers. So it was after the war, Arly come back, Lauerence sends him and his brother out to my place—well the home-place there—teach 'em how to farm. Nora, she's home from Fargo for awhile. Yeah. Well, she didn't go back to Fargo very much after that! Course I was always after her to stick around here, so that worked out too. Couldn't find a better man! That's a fact. Yes sir—that is a fact!

So the story ran again through his head, but it broke off…

Also in George's mind during the visit that afternoon was the clear fact that Lauerence would not be recovering, and an antique pity stirred as his own thoughts failed momentarily to keep that fact at bay—It was clear—he had always known—Lauerence was the weak one. All the times George found him that way…It started right after she died, the epidemic, everyone wearing white masks, afraid to breath. Lauerence didn't leave the house for a week after the funeral. Then he got better, went back to work, then six months later it happened again. Everyone left him alone—that's what he wanted. Sitting there in the dark day after day. Couple years later he got married again, then the spells, or whatever they were, went away for awhile.

Nothing I could do. Next time he got so he wouldn't even eat—just smoke cigarette after cigarette all alone there in the dark. Wouldn't talk to anyone. That's when we started sending him away. Doctor's fixed him up or something, then he was back. Every couple of years, the same thing then. Nothing I could do.

All the old images came back, and George stood as if suddenly confronted by the sepulchral white of the room, it's complete silence offering him no refuge from the forbidding sense of loneliness flooding through him now, because there was nothing else but the loneliness of wasted lives here echoing back, this dead room looking across this dead land, the silence of one speaking to the silence of the other. He was alone. Lauerence was alone. It was always the same. Nothing he could do would ever change that. Especially now. It would always be too late forever and ever.

The grass outside the window was ready to burn up. Have to buy plenty more hay. Maybe put in another well. You get better—take you out there. Show you I can do it—show 'em all. I can raise horses—set up a whole rodeo—you know kids come from all over the county just to ride my horses. Gonna build a show barn—biggest indoor rodeo in the state. Got a fellow workin' on it. I got plans—you see. Big plans. Gonna show everyone. Fellow out in Montana says he wants to sell me a hundred Appaloosas, so I 'm thinkin about that too. And cars too, why I'm tradin' left and right—I'm a wheeler dealer you know. Can't set still—do nothin', why I got girlfriends all around this state—I'll tell you a thing or two about that…

Lauerence would not be waking up again for a long time. George had crept away hours ago, closed the door quietly behind him, gone back for awhile to another land.

He slept in his chair until dark when the attendants appeared and hoisted him into the bed. They adjusted the sheets around his face, emptied the garbage, switched on a yellow "help" light by the door, then left.

He laid awake staring into the dark for a long time. What muffled voices there had once been faded completely. It was cold, colder than usual. Just like that. Yes.

There could be so much snow sometimes it was hard to believe. They could have just left me there. Just leave me. Just go away. Oh yeah. Just tired. That's all. You don't understand.

He reached out trembling for his cigarettes on the night table. Working very carefully with slow, deliberate moves, he put a cigarette into his mouth, then with a single precise strike, lit a match, touched the flame to the tobacco, then let the still-lit match drop from his fingers to the sheets…

The attendants were able to smother the fire in time—only by luck one of them happened to be passing by the room and smelled smoke…

Arly's habit settled into periodic evening visits. He read the paper and paced the hallways, then read the paper some more. Sometimes Nora came as well as the boys. Tip would study and Jim would put a puzzle together.

By late September Lauerence was gaining some control over his speech again—a slurred unintelligible whisper interpreted by Schadow as a good sign, much to everyone's relief. His progress lent an especially festive atmosphere to the fiftieth wedding anniversary party in October. Lauerence was even strong enough then to cut his own piece of cake with Grandma Kern's help. He smiled in all the pictures and full recovery was expected.

He died on Christmas day. Arly was the first to receive the call. The body would be shipped to Madrid—Mort Wirt, the mortician there, would take charge of it. He would need to go over some details with a member of the family and he'd be calling later.

They ate. Grandma and Grandpa Sedler, who arrived just after the call, left again soon after the meal. Around three, Wirt called; Arly told the boys to take care of the chores, drove across town to pick up Will, then headed through the White Hills to the mortuary in Madrid. It was twilight when they arrived.

They hadn't said a word until they got to town, then Will looked up at the lights and the wreaths strung across mainstreet—the wind had grown wicked and it tossed them back and forth with a savage force—"Pretty here," he said, his cigarette hand pointing skyward. "Every year, seems to get more and more lights."

"Yeah. That's…"

Wirt welcomed them with his meaty, consolatory face, his handshake registering both the sympathy and professionalism that had made him famous throughout the area. He didn't hold himself aloof either, not like a lot of the others—he liked to mingle, and the joke was that if he wouldn't have been such a good mortician, he'd make a fine mayor. He should consider running.

There was a list of platitudes, then they all settled into his leather office to look through the catalogs spread out across the desk. Will let his brother do the talking, nodding mechanical assent to all the decisions. Mahogany. Velvet. Titanium.

All the way home, Will wept.

The funeral was in St. Anthony's Missouri Synod, the white, wooden country church south of town, just at the edge of the Hills. The bitter wind howled and shook the windows, driving the snow, dry as salt, in snakelike swirls across the open plain. The organist played out the last of his wheezing, mournful chords and the crippled Father Verdrehen wound his way into the pulpit that hovered above the hundred shivering mourners—his eyes, black beads magnified and swimming in glassy pools, so as he peered down, it was as a hunchbacked bird-man guarding a craggy nest. His eyes registered prey and he swooped down for the attack.

"The flesh is foul—it rots and blows away. The flesh is but sin, it is the sin we carry with us, the sin which enshrouds our soul from the time that we are born to the time that we die. It is finally in death that we are able to cast aside our sinful nature and be free of it. Certainly the flesh gives us pleasure—it is pleasant to eat and it is pleasant to work, to feel our labor as it wears us down, and then it is pleasant to sleep. But God did not put us on earth so that we may merely lose ourselves in such pleasures, he gave us flesh so that we may know sin, so that we can be strengthened by our resistance to sin, by our resistance to the pleasures of the flesh.

"Flesh is our burden, it is the heavy shroud we wear all our lives, the shroud worn by Lauerence Kern which he has now cast off, left behind on a sinful earth so that his soul can depart freely to dwell forever in the bosom of his Lord.

"And it is God who will judge Lauerence, who will weigh his life in the justice of his own hands and who will determine his eternal fate; it is to God he comes just as it is to God that all of us must come to be judged. Did we wear our flesh too proudly? If so, God will judge us harshly. Did we idle away our time in fruitless pleasure? If so, God will judge us harshly. Did we put too much stock in this earthly life? If so, God will judge us harshly. God detests the proud. We know that. God detests the pleasure-seekers. We know that. God detests the flesh. We know that.

"But in his wisdom, he gave us this flesh to test us, to test our souls. Many of us must fail this test. We will become mired in sin and will find no way out. When this happens, God is saddened, and he is also angered, for the law of eternal justice demands punishment for such weak souls—eternal punishment in painful, burning hellfire—he does not want to condemn, but he must. Yes. The flesh is foul. It must rot and blow away."

The organist played "Jacob's Ladder" as Father Verdrehen descended and took his place behind the altar. The service continued, the church growing colder and colder—the tiny furnace in the basement incapable of fighting back the twenty below weather that had been reigning all December. With the concluding chords of the final hymn, the pall bearers took up their burden and loaded it into the hearse. The congregation then made its way across the swirling waste to the cemetery, following the body on its quarter mile trek to the back gates. Because of his crooked spine, Father Verdrehen had to be driven to the graveside. He gave one last message.

"God, we commend into your hands the soul of Lauerence Kern. His flesh is here in the earth. May his soul dwell with you forever and ever."

The black line of mourners writhed its way back to the church basement where vats of hamburger and macaroni hotdish awaited them as well as plates of shimmering green Jell-O salad flecked with bits of lettuce, and as everyone inched their way along the steam table, the cooks ladled out generous scoopfulls of the funeral fare.

A few people took off their coats, but kept their sweaters tightly buttoned. Those still in their coats jokingly called them "the brave ones."

The immediate family sat together at one long table. Arly kept his coat tightly buttoned, as did the rest of the family. No one spoke. George couldn't eat—he sat in silence as the hotdish cooled into a yellow greasy pool on his plate. His eyes stared unfocused. Grandma Sedler and her daughter exchanged occasional whispers along with Grandma Kern, next to Nora, who especially admired the salad. They all agreed the cooks had done a good job. Arly and Will sat together. Suddenly Will let out a deep sob and couldn't stop. Arly, his fork frozen in his hand, stared at his brother out of the corner of his eye. A few other eyes at nearby tables glanced up, then quickly looked away.

When his sobbing subsided, Will lit a cigarette, got up and left. The cooks came by with second helpings and fresh pots of coffee. Soon after that, the basement emptied and everyone hurried off to their idling cars, exhaust tearing away like white sheets rent by the bitter wind.

As the cars scattered into the countryside, Wirt pushed a button on the grave-lift and lowered the casket. He motioned to his two assistants. They aimed the fuel oil heaters at the mound of frozen dirt. The heaters were plugged into a portable generator and soon they were blazing away, baking out the ice.

There was nothing but silence and shadows as the last of the car lights faded into the hills. The three men worked away with their picks, their coat collars turned up against the cold, twilight turning quickly into night as the unbounded prairie was sheeted with driven snow, and soon again there was no shadow left of tree or twig to break the fixed trance of whiteness: lean ice monuments and splintered crosses rising through the desolate shiftings of the windrowed snow in dumb blankness, but this time without meaning, without meaning and without end.

Chapter Ten

Will scooped another five pounds of ground pork into the tub on the floor, then he measured out a palmful of mustard seed and spread it in concentric circles over the mixture. He knelt beside the tub then and kneaded the meat and the mustard seed together.

"What you gotta think is," he said, "Is that we can fry up a patty of this on the stove to see how it tastes now, and it might taste all right, but you gotta think down the line a ways, how it's gonna be after its been hanging in the smokehouse for a couple of weeks and all the flavors change on you—that's what we're really after. So how it tastes now isn't the thing, it's how it gonna taste later that counts, 'cause once it's made and it's smoked, that's it—we're stuck with it all winter."

He explained his philosophy to Jim, gesturing with his cigarette now as he leaned against the edge of the stove. "Winter can be a long time to go too. Yeah, you always gotta think what it's gonna be like later on."

He stubbed his cigarette out in the ashtray, washed his hands, then molded up a couple patties from the mixture and tossed them into the black iron skillet on the stove.

When the patties were browned, Will handed samples all around. Jim popped one of the savory morsels into his mouth. It tasted like autumn, and winter too. He played with the mustard seeds in his mouth.

Will went back to work—seven more pounds of ground beef , some coarse black pepper and more mustard.

He worked the spices through again and cooked up some more patties.

"There." He said. "Now we got it!" He ate another bite. "Pete, we're in business."

Pete was Will's nickname for his nephew—Jim didn't know where the name came from, but it made him feel good when he heard it.

While these last adjustments were being made, Nora and her sister in law, Esther, bolted the sausage-maker to the edge of the kitchen table. It was a heavy silver machine with a funnel on top for the meat, a wooden crank on the side and a smooth polished tube on the front where the sausage was pumped out into the casing.

The casings were pork; an enormous silver bowlful of them stood in the sink massed in a slick, clean, milk-white pile. It would be Jim's job to slip the casing onto the tube and hold it tight there with his hand while Julie, his cousin, turned the crank that pressed out the meat. Nora tied off the sausages in foot long links, cut them with a scissors, then Esther tied the two ends together into a ring. Will and Arly kept the meat coming in scoopfulls and packing it into the funnel. It was the same system every fall.

Arly joked with his brother as they carted the meat, and he even joked with Julie about turning the crank and getting muscles like Popeye. It surprised Jim to hear his father laugh; he didn't know what to make of it. It made him nervous.

Jim and Julie would look at one another and smile every once in a while, though neither of them said much. They were both intent on their jobs, but Jim's fingers started to get cold and slimy, and it was harder and harder for him to hold the casings in place over the tube until finally his fingers slipped off and the meat oozed out all over.

"Better let her do that for awhile," His father said, motioning to Julie with his scoop.

They switched places.

"Gotta turn it just so now. Be careful. Slow. Slow. Slower." his father instructed.

Julie looked at Jim and rolled her eyes. Bitchy Itchy Arly.

The silver tub on the floor was steadily filling with the finished rings.

By the end of the afternoon there would be three tubs filled, then there'd be a trip to Blake Cripes smokehouse down by the Sand Hills; two weeks later the rings would be wrapped in white packages and stacked in the freezer in the store. Once or twice a week then all winter there would be sausage for supper, served, according to custom, with only white bread and grape jelly.

You cooked the sausage in a shallow pan of water, and just before it was ready to eat, you'd lift up the lid of the pan and sneak the tip of a knife inside to puncture the skin and let the grease and the juices out. The skin was so tight that the liquid could shoot clear across the kitchen if you weren't careful, so you had to hold the cover just so.

That was the main reason why Arly would always officiate over the proceedings, careful to perform all the surgical cuts with nervous precision.

It was also important to know how to slip your fork under the skin, then rip it open and roll the meat out—it would always come off clean and steamy if you did it just right. The mustard seeds would be especially soft and the grape jelly was the perfect contrast for the hot, salty, smoky taste.

"Better go up—the store, gotta check something," Arly said. He set his scoop down and grabbed his hat. "Gettin' dark."

Will glanced up at him over his glasses. "You want to go out to Cripes with me then or what?"

"Don't know. No. You go on. I gotta talk to – tire woman – Seneca – what's her name? New order."

He left.

"Well, What d'ya say Pete? You wanta come with then?"

Jim had been to the Sand Hills only a handful of times, and the chance to go there with his uncle was more than he could believe, but soon they were lifting the tubs into the pick up box and the two of them were headed out of town.

Will lit a cigarette, settled back behind the steering wheel and turned the heater on. "Yeah. It's gonna be a good winter for sausage."

It was getting late in the afternoon. The autumn air was sharp and crisp. They crossed the railroad tracks south of town and drove past the baseball field—its set of wooden bleachers and two wooden dugouts. The bleachers and the dugouts were painted green but the paint was always crumbling, and the roofs of the dugouts were bowed and warped from rain and snow. The home run fence was a rickety wooden snow fence, and behind that was a cornfield.

On gamenights the town would be filled with people; cars were parked everywhere up and down the streets and all along the ditches. He was allowed to go to the game as long as he was with Tip, and he sat in the weeds under the scoreboard with his brother and brother's friends. They kept score with wooden squares with red numbers painted on them. The squares were scattered all around on the ground. It was Jim's job to get them ready for his brother to use.

It was impossible to understand the game, but he liked getting caught up in the excitement when someone scored or when there was a home run. Tip always gave him a dime for popcorn—Ray Hektner and his kids sold it in greasy brown paper bags stacked up in the trunk of his car.

Ray had the only popcorn machine around; he kept it in his service station, and whenever Jim had to run an errand there, and while Ray disappeared into the backroom to get the belt or the bearing or whatever it was the boy was sent for, he would find himself standing in front of the machine, studying it—the piles of stale popcorn banked up in back, the battered black salt shaker, the thick black layers of grease on the popper itself.

The bright silver base was covered with clowns and acrobats, and on top ran a row of yellow light bulbs: a dark carnival surrounded by used tires, cobwebs and tubes of grease.

They crossed the bridge over the Wild Rice. It was running shallow and the clay banks were hollowed out and crumbling. Immediately, the land changed. The road no longer cut straight—it curved and climbed steeply, winding its way through marshes and gullies, and as it did so it narrowed into a single lane. The ditches were deep, brimming with cattails. Red wing blackbirds sang out in bright trills, holding their last note as if playing it through broken reeds, tremulous but still clear.

They drove past St. Anthony's and the cemetery where Grandpa Kern was buried. There were so many graves, it was impossible to tell now where his grandfather was as they drove past.

Will had grown silent since they crossed the river; he also scanned the headstones now.

"That's where your grandpa is, you know."

Jim nodded, remembering the funeral. It was the only time he'd ever seen his uncle cry and it startled him. It was the first time he'd seen anyone cry, unless it was when someone fell down and hurt themselves on the playground. He knew he cried too whenever they chased him and beat him, but that was different.

"You probably don't remember him very well when he was still pretty healthy. He was pretty sick, you know, the last five or six years. I was always taking him to the doctor for one thing or another. He wasn't really ever in the best of health."

Will would not be elaborating. He was losing himself in his own memories growing up—Great Grandpa Kern's house—stairways, gables—porch on the third floor closed off now thirty years—the whole house more and more closed off every year.

Great Grandpa Kern. Gruff German. Only spoke it with Great-grandma Kern. Spoke English with everyone else, or tried to.

Her. Voice shaking. Always on the verge of tears. Crippled hands in her lap wringing out the hours. Eyes staring out over the top of Maples Groves in the third floor study—the one with the porch. Hardly left the room. Books. Piano. Every once in a while a note or two plucked out, then a terrible crashing. Something had fallen. One day they found her on the floor.

Great-Grandpa Kern lived only a few years more than she did. Lauerence gave the piano to the opera hall, then a few years after that, he took all the books out into the backyard and burned them.

"Look at that," Will pointed.

A flock of geese cut a V through the gray air.

"Just think, if we were birds, that's where we'd be now."

Jim smiled.

"You know, I could just sit and watch the birds all day," Will said. "How about you?"

"Yeah." He blushed.

Soon the road became little more than a fence-lined path, the last rays of the fading sun filtering through the rich mosaic reds, yellows and golds above. Then what was left of the path disappeared entirely into the slough itself just as they turned and followed the long twisting driveway that led to Blake Cripes' farm. Above them now tree branches grew together in a black-knit canopy that made the driveway already dark as night, and around the trees themselves crouched the rusty remains of antique machinery—cornheads, horse-drawn rakes, the looming silver carcass of a threshing machine that had seen its last season twenty or thirty years ago.

Dozens of other unidentifiable relics rose up eerily out of the dark, and the driveway seemed to go on forever; then finally, the odor of wood smoke, a rooster darted across the road, and at last the trees gave way to a vast farmyard.

But what years ago had been prosperous was now littered with derelict buildings patched together by crumbling brick and mismatched lumber, and just as they pulled into the yard, Blake, the last unwashed, grizzled, bachelor survivor of the Cripes dynasty, spat out a rattling chain of tobacco juice through a toothless smile.

"So what you boys come to steal?" Came his barbed-wire voice as Will climbed out of the truck and ground his cigarette out under his boot.

"Depends on what you got." Will said.

"Got everything you need, long as you don't need much. Tell you though, just got three cords of hickory put up, so I figure I got enough to smoke half the meat in Ashkenaz County if I care to—yes sir, the whole blame Ash-can-ass county."

"We'll settle for just fifty rings worth."

"Fair enough. Who's the boy?"

"That's my nephew, Jim."

"So you ridin' shotgun today, Jim?"

Jim nodded, his face turning bright red. As Will and Blake talked he stood mesmerized by all the windowless buildings, the door frames without doors, and all the walls and roofs covered with bright moss. There were a lot of run-down farms in the county but not one so completely, almost artfully decayed.

The house rose two and a half stories with a full porch on the first and second floor; the railing on the second floor porch was twisting and hanging off the side in pieces, and the black hole behind it was a little taller than the two black holes on either side of it. The burned-out hulk of a car—a Packard or something like it—stood beside the house, and next to that was a chicken coop with an oak tree growing out of the windows and doors. The coop had broken off its foundation, and it was inching away year after year, riding the branches skyward.

The machine shed was surrounded by scrap metal—piles of radiators, tire rims, boiler plate, engine blocks, feeder chains, log chains, straw walkers and anything else that could rust. Next to the machine shed there was a barn that had once been painted red with white trim and hayloft doors that had once been opened wide in antique summer suns. Now it was all kneeling slowly into the earth, its spine split.

Everywhere, jagged plates of shingles littered the ground curling like snake skins scraped off by the wind. And everywhere machinery stood on blocks or was suspended by ropes from tree branches or homemade sky-hooks.

"So Jim, you know your uncle here is the most famous sausage-maker around, don't you!"

Blake nudged the boy good-naturedly.

Will spoke. "No. I tell you what, Blake. It was Grandpa Kern I learned it from.

"Yeah. Too damn bad he had to die like that. Well, you know, my dad knew your dad, and your grand-dad. Everyone used to make it themselves. That was a long time ago. Not many folks makin' it at all anymore."

Will drew out a cigarette and cupped a flame in his hand.

Blake looked up at the sky. "It's all changed. New world."

"Yeah, Blake," he said, "That is a fact." He tossed the match to the ground. "But you either move or get run over."

"Well, that's me. Been run over so many times…A man's just gotta stop, you know, and figure it all out. Just that, when I was a boy, I thought things would work out different. So here they are. Pretty dif-fernt." He threw his head back and laughed. Will offered a sad cigarette gesture of silent agreement.

They hauled the tubs up to the smokehouse, Blake chanting, "Tub of guts! Tub of guts!" He lit a kerosene lantern and hung it on a nail just inside the door. Pale yellow light illuminated the smoke and all the meat hanging up on the racks. The smell of hickory filled the air.

Chapter Eleven

Jim cut through Isaac Johnson's lot: he had disobeyed—his parents had gone to Lake Cocytus with Dick and Anna Lee, and he wasn't supposed to leave the yard—but the desire for adventure was too strong; it outweighed all fear of punishment. He was going to the river. Since the previous Autumn with Will, he'd been there only once, fishing with his brothers on Easter Sunday—although he couldn't fish, he just stood on the bank and watched. If he was patient, he thought then, he would be rewarded with a day like this.

He headed across the tracks south of town. All around him the cannibalized carcasses of old engines and freight cars loomed up out of the weeds. Seagulls fed on stray grain along the rails. He looked back at all the crumbling houses and abandoned stores. A dog barked. The smell of creosote rose from the ties. Except for the gulls, there wasn't a trace of movement anywhere along the broken streets and weed-choked alleys.

The elevator loomed above him—a vast brick monolith, "1900" carved high up at the top, a tombstone over the Sunday silence—then beyond that, the open country—field after field after field until the land met the sky seamlessly shifting gold to blue then back again.

He took the path along Lahmung's fence line, stubble fields on both sides. It was a fine Autumn day—flocks of geese far above etching the blue sky with their fluid V's, and far above that, a jet's vapor trail bending sunward.

Ravens rose then landed again in black ripples across the fields. Their cries, the cry of the gulls, and the cool breeze now and then that rustled gently across the stubble were the only sounds, and he listened for how they blended together, one sound becoming another.

He paused beside a stand of cottonwoods to examine the remains of a walking plow, a Scotch Clipper. Its oak handles worn smooth and its moldboard covered in rust: abandoned one day, the horses unhitched, led off by some farmer; the horses and the farmer had long ago ridden again into their own dust, but that day he left it—did he know then? He must have thought he would be returning, or assumed that he would be, but never did. The plow was still here, the rusty testament of a moment's labor, though its bones too crumbling, only slower than the man's.

A few more steps brought him to the ragged clay bank of the river. He peered over the edge. The Wild Rice, a serpentine ribbon never more than twenty feet across, meandered a turgid and brown course through the heart of Ashkenaz County. Beneath him, a crude dam checked the level—only a trickle sluiced over the stones now—and on the other side a pasture of rolling hills and vast groves stretched to the horizon, the emerald grass touching the blue outline of the Sand Hills.

By a clump of willows, their silver vines dangling in the river, half a dozen Hereford cows rested in the shade. Calves pranced in long-legged gambols through the cascading branches. Every once in a while a calf would scramble off to its mother, nudge her with its pink nose, then take off again as if inciting her to play, but she would only look on with her white face and enormous brown eyes, gently swaying her head in response.

On one of the higher hills stood a threshing machine, its grain spout extended—a dinosaur frozen in time, its neck stretched to feed on long-disappeared branches. He remembered pictures of dinosaurs from school—they had lived here millions of years ago, then after they died and the glaciers melted the entire valley was a lake called Lake Agassiz. It was a thousand feet deep and it was here for thousands of years. He lived at the bottom of a lake—or it was more like a sea because that was another name for it—The Inland Sea.

The county was covered with fossils. Will pointed one out to Jim on their land down by Weed. On a boulder the size of a pickup were the raised bones of fishlike creatures with flat heads and sinuous spines winding in wild contortions, swimming in stone, still feeding.

A bullhead jumped, splashing back into the water. If you looked up at the sky long enough you could see to the end of the universe, and if you thought about time long enough you could go all the way back to the beginning. You'd have to be patient, because it would take forever to do that kind of work, and you couldn't do anything else except look and think because that's how much time it would take. It was important to know where things ended and where things began. Then you'd know…well, first you'd have to find out about it all. You'd have to look and think and look and think and look and think, and then you'd know. It all comes back but it comes back in stone.

He looked off to the north. In the distance, the grain elevator and the church steeple rose above the trees: two poles sticking up, the town suspended between them.

Last month was his first confession: looking at the steeple now reminded him of that evening he returned home, feeling cleansed, then his father speaking to him from the living room: "Where you been?" and in three simple words irreparably violating his new sense of piety, making it dirty, destroying the feeling, and under his breath he cursed his father, who, he realized was probably only trying to make conversation, but it failed. It always failed. For that he cursed his father again.

It was early evening; the sky was dark with the rain that had been falling all day. He made his fast, just as Father Misere instructed, he reviewed his sins, then he ran off to the church—lightning flashing in the distance, thunder rolling overhead.

He touched his fingers to the font, crossed himself, then made his way down the aisle, above him, rain pattering the roof.

The only thing darker than the gloom inside the church was the light cast into it. He knelt with all the other penitents and waited his turn, staring up at the green and blue mosaics filled with crucifixions, weeping, heads either bowed in prayer or cast expectantly heavenward, and what light broke through all these heavenly pains seemed there only to darken them and to mock the penitents—a huddled few of them who had finished their penance moving off to an alcove—gray web-faced figures kneeling in the feeble red of the votive candles—from penance to mourning, they pushed their quarters through the slot, lit a new candle from the flame of one already burning, and bowed their heads…

Bless me Father for I have sinned.

The shadow of a hand in the sign of the cross.

How long has it been since your last confession?

This is my first confession, Father.

Another shadow crossed the smoky glass.

In what ways, then, have you sinned?

“I said some bad words, and I stole some money, and I've had bad thoughts about people.”

“These bad words, were they said in anger?”

Yes, Father.”

“You must learn to control your anger, then. And the money, can you put it back?”

“Yes, Father.”

“Then you should put it back. Someone earned that money, you see, and if you steal money without working for it, it hurts that person. Do you understand?”

“Yes, Father.”

“Now, these bad thoughts. Were they about someone in your family?”

“Yes, Father.”

“Your family loves you very much. If your parents ask you to do something and you don't want to, you should remember that they're only trying to teach you how to do things for yourself. Do you have bad thoughts about them?"

"Yes, Father."

"Then, as I said, you should know it is a sin to have bad thoughts, and if it's against your parents, it is an especially bad sin against them. Do you have bad thoughts about others in your family?"

"Yes, Father."

"I see. Do you have any sisters?"

"No, Father."

"Ah, only brothers."

"Yes, Father."

"Sometimes brothers argue. It's only natural. Is that what you do, do you argue?"

"Yes, Father."

"And then you have bad thoughts?"

"Yes, Father."

"What kind of bad thoughts? Is there something else?"

"No, Father."

"Are there any other sins for which you are seeking absolution?"

Jim thought. "I stole some pears off a pear tree."

Father Misere was silent for a long time. Jim thought that he might not have heard, and was about to repeat his sin when the priest finally said, "And why did you do that?"

"They looked good, so I took some."

"Well, that's perfectly understandable. But still, you gave into temptation, and that is always a sin. Do you understand?"

"Yes, Father."

The priest paused. Jim felt the ache in his knees, and his fingers were locked so tightly together that they had begun to hurt as well, but he was afraid to move. He was hot and dizzy and wanted to run away, but he was trapped there. Father Misere knew who he was. That was certain now. Maybe he wasn't sure at first—that must be why he asked about sisters—he wasn't sure at first, but now he knew. Were these sins? What was sin? A sin was a bad thought...

For your penance say three Hail Marries. In the name of the father and the son and the holy spirit, I absolve you of all your sins. Go in peace.

Sin. Punishment. Reward. Father Misere's outline on the blackboard. It was raining that day too. Mass afterwards. Sinful thoughts lead to sinful deeds. We must be punished for both. Because Adam and Eve sinned we must be punished with death. After our punishment we will be rewarded with life everlasting.

He had disobeyed. But he had no choice. He had to leave. He would be punished, but there would be no reward. This was his reward. His sin was his reward.

He didn't like thinking about sin.

Now and at the hour of our death ...

Forgive us our trespasses...

She gave him a tablespoon of vitamins, then watched him as he knelt at the bedside, his hands folded. The door pulled shut. He climbed under the covers. His head was filled with images of Hell—there were so many sins...Thinking about Hell now brought the taste of his mother's brown liquid dosing to his tongue.

If he jumped into the river he'd go straight to Hell. That was a fact. How do fish breathe underwater? Fish have gills. Yes. That's right. Fish have gills. She always answered all the questions. She would just raise her hand and answer. She was pretty and her legs were pretty and she had nice long blonde hair.

He wanted to talk to her but it was impossible. They could live together in a cabin on the river.

Too many thoughts were flooding in. He felt dizzy. He closed his eyes tightly and held them shut for a long time. When he opened them the first thing he saw was a daddy long legs crawling over his shoe. He swatted at the spider, then crushed it. A cold shiver went through him. He'd have to go home soon.

He looked off to the town again. All the houses were hidden or obscured by the trees. Some of the trees were changing already. The first one to change was called the Judas tree—a sudden burst of orange and yellow among all the solid banks of green. After awhile they'd all turn so they'd all become Judas trees. Why was it only the first one that counted? Black branches surrounded by gray, the gray turning to white, the water turning to ice, one thing becoming another until everything was dead again…

He stood and started the long walk home. They'd be back by now. He stayed away too long. The sky was darkening to the west. Already fine gray streaks brushed the horizon—rain heading his way. The streaks alarmed him and he started running, stumbling over the uneven ground. It was getting colder by the minute, the wind turning sharply bitter. His coat, zipped to the collar now, offered little protection.

By the time he got to the elevator, the rain had started, falling at first in great explosions in the dust like spiders that came smashing down from out of the black clouds, and soon, with only two blocks to go, he couldn't even see through the downpour; it was already washing away a deep gully beside the burnt remains of the old cream station, and as he splashed through it's sudden river, taking the shortcut home, he stumbled and fell.

He half-expectantly thought someone would come by and help him up, but no one did. He realized it made no sense—there was no one here. No one at all. Shivering and frightened he picked himself up and was soon feeling his way through the willow branches at the edge of the yard. There was a light in the living room, the curtains drawn aside, his father's bleary outline at the window.

The instant Jim touched the door it flew back on its hinges. His mother's long black hair fell in tangled dripping streaks across her face. Shrieking, "Where have you been? Where have you been?" over and over, she stood, her hand raised, ready to strike. Her green eyes trapped him there, casting forth an insane green glow as her hand fell, over and over, "Where have you been? Where have you been…"

Chapter Twelve

In the heart of the winter now, Lake Cocytus was a thick frozen sheet of glass swept by wind and snow, and scattered across it, fisherman squatting froglike, their faces bowed toward the ice, each of them testifying to the cold with their chattering mouths, their eyes tearing constantly—hunch-backed, unmoving, and stolid, the livid dead sealed in place. They kept their heat in a bottle and they ate their fish raw. At night they pulled the ice over their shoulders and slept, tears freezing their eyelids shut.

A handful of fish houses dotted the ice as well, and in the center of the lake stood the Kern's house, its gas lantern spilling yellow light through tiny square windows as dusk gathered around it and gray clouds drew down through the gray air in a sullen twilight fog.

The door swung open, a silver trout fluttered across the ice, joining the half dozen other already stiffened bodies there, and the same hand that had released it plucked a wine bottle from the snow and slammed the door shut again. There were only four people inside, Arly and Nora, and their friends, Bob and Anna Lee, but they'd been fishing and drinking all afternoon and were making enough noise for forty people. A similar nimbus of guffaws and farting laughter radiated from practically every other house on the ice; however, The Kerns and the Schluckers had been at it longer than anyone else and were especially radiant this evening.

"I'm a easy target I suppose, Huh?" Bob said.

Oh c'mon, nobody's laughin' at you!" Anna Lee said.

"Oh yeah! Nobody's laughin'—old Bob!"

"Well only when you make yourself ridiculous."

"Maybe—like makin' myself ridiculous. Maybe dat's what I like—do. Maybe dat's all—know *how* to do! I'm a artist, you see!"

"Oh yeah, you're a artist all right! You turned me from a Schlumpe to a Schlucker and all you had to do was turn on the old charm machine, wave your magic wand…"

"Dat's right, me an' my magic wand! *Me* and my *magic* wand!"

"C'mon!" Arly cut in. "Schlumpe, you just need—Schnapps!" He slammed the bottle down on the arm of Bob's chair, laughing at his own joke.

"What's dis?" Bob said, taking a swig from the bottle then passing it back. "What's dis now, got me somethin' on—line. Loo—a—dis now…"

Arly eyed the line growing taut then slack then taut again. "What you got, little perch playin' with you again. Now me, what I'm after—the great big ones!"

"Arly's gonna catch himself a whale!" Anna Lee shouted.

"That's right! Gonna catch me a whale! Exactly what I'm after! Gonna get—pull it right up—bottom of the lake. Fish all day, all night!"

"Well before you get too involved," Nora said, "Fix me another drink."

"You're on the hard stuff today, aren't you?" Anna Lee chided.

"Girl's gotta stay warm somehow."

"We got enough heat in here, why we're just gonna explode aren't we!" Anna Lee said, finishing her glass and pouring another.

"Better not," Arly said. "Scare all the fish away!"

"Shhh. Shhh. That's right,"Nora said, putting her finger to her lips and whispering, "Everyone be very quiet. Don't say anything."

And for whatever reason, everyone was quiet for awhile.

Bob dug into his pocket and produced a stubby little black pipe which he refilled with pungent black tobacco. He touched a match to it and was soon exhaling meditative plumes as he played with his line in the water, letting it slip through blackened fingers, then tugging at it, then letting it slip. As usual, for the winter, he had grown his beard full again and added another twenty pounds or so to his already broad girth. His deep set eyes, intensely magnified by his thick horn-rimmed glasses, gazed into the smoke as if puzzling out something from its amorphous riddling banks.

Tracing circles with her finger around the rim of her wine glass, Anna Lee stared through the hole in the ice in which her own line was dangling. The wine was having just the right effect. Whenever the four of them got together there were so many parts to

play…It was easy to get lost, but that was half the fun. It was something to do. After all, what else was there? Nothing. Nothing. Nothing. Nothingness. Nothing thing. No thing. Thing at all. Too bad about her.

It was all held in place by the tension of the unsaid, and so long as the proper silences were respected there wouldn't be any trouble. She took a sip and glanced up at Arly, who was crouching over his tackle box, searching for something in the tiny compartments. Yes, too bad.

Arly noticed her glance and smiled, blushing. He hooked a berry weighter to his line and dropped it back down the hole. He studied the exposed wall of smooth ice – air bubbles trapped there like wheat straws fanned out, a shock of frozen wheat. He could stay there all winter. The hell with everything else. She shouldn't look at him like that though. It wasn't right.

Nora rolled her glass back and forth between her hands, then glanced at their coats lined up on hooks dangling from the ceiling. "Like wearing a ton of lead all winter."

"What?" Anna Lee asked.

"Our coats. Look at them. Who'd want to live in a place where you have to go around in a ton of lead just to stay warm?"

"I guess we're doing it."

"Well I'm sick of it. Sometimes I think I'd just as soon freeze to death and get it over with."

"Dat's not a bad way to go – Dat's what I hear, anyway," Bob added through the smoke. "Get so cold, you see, you get hot, so you take – clothes off, an' I guess you jus get hotter an' hotter till you freeze to death."

"That's stupid," Anna Lee said.

"Dat's jus' what I hear, dat's all. I don't know."

"I never heard such a stupid thing."

"I'll tell you what's stupid," Nora said. "Junkers, North Dakota. *That's* stupid. What a dump."

"What's that from?" Anna Lee asked. "It sounds like it from something."

"It's from a movie. A Bette Davis movie."

"That's what I thought! You always know all these movies…And opera. I can't believe you listen to opera."

"Why not? What am I supposed to listen to?"

"Oh, I don't know."

"It makes more sense than what a lot of other people do around here."

"I wouldn't know about that. Oh I don't know. Sure, Junkers is no great shakes of a place…"

"No great shakes is right! There's more ghosts around here than anything. More dead people around here than there are living. And if this great mayor I'm married too would *do* anything, he'd make people clean up the place. There's more abandoned houses full of bums and drunks than anything."

"Oh, come on now," Arly said. "Private property – pay their taxes, can't touch it."

"You could if you wanted to."

"Let's not get into that now."

"More ghosts around here than anything. That's what it is. A ghost town. Nothing but. It's humiliating living here."

"I wouldn't know about that either," Anna Lee said.

"Well it is. It's absolutely humiliating. I feel like I might as well just be ghost too. Maybe I am already."

By this time the other three had stopped listening to her. She smiled to herself and finished her glass. "Just the dead talking. So what? You see it all the time."

Arly's line snapped tight. "Got one!" He ejaculated. "Got one!" He kept yelling as he hauled it in hand over hand.

"Arly got himself a whale!" Anna Lee shrieked.

But suddenly the line went limp. "Damn!," He said, disgusted. "That was—big one too! Could feel it!"

"A regular whale! Arly had himself a regular whale, he did!"

"Too big. Too smart—that's—trouble."

"You'll get him! You'll get him back all right!"

"Oh yaaa! I—I stake my stick on – at on that! One thing—sure of!" Bob said.

Nora stared into the blackening water. Night was coming on fast. She was able to concentrate on little more than her disgust for the whole situation, and it continued to manifest itself in diatribes against Junkers.

"Infernal dump in the sticks. I don't know why anyone has to feel like they need to defend it. Just look at it for what it is. Junky town. Junky people."

"People, way I see…" Bob trailed off, distracted by his line. "Make – own—Hell. Way I see it…Way I see it…" But his line was too strong an attraction, forcing him to give up philosophy altogether.

"You ain't never happy," Arly mumbled, surprised his voice actually surfaced—it was only a thought—he didn't mean to be heard.

"No. I guess I'm not, am I? I guess I'm just not very good at living a second rate life in a no rate town."

"Oh—drop it already."

"I will not drop it. Why pretend we're living someplace we're not? That's just childish. It's called Junkers for a reason. It's not called Paradise, and it's not even Purgatory—of course you wouldn't know about that!" Her green eyes cast a venomous glow at Arly as if they would burn through him.

"You should have known that before you married the old coot!" Anna Lee laughed.

"What's that supposed to mean?"

"Oh come on! I'm just making a joke. You're making everyone nervous, the way you talk. Let's have some fun! Come on! Of course it's not the greatest town on earth, but so what?"

Nora threw her rod to the floor, tore her coat from the hook and stormed outside into the cold, slamming the door defiantly behind her.

Insect goes away and dies. Duty done. Freeze here. There he comes now. It's not so cold. I can lie with the best of them.

She continued walking across the ice, enveloped in a gray fog. Above, the starless sky augured no direction for her to follow. It didn't matter. She would just keep walking. Only vanity made her think there ever would be anything else. Her eyes teared up from the cold and the tears froze to her face, her gaze fixed straight ahead. Every once in a while she cast a glance skyward. The gray black ceiling closed in deeper and darker as she disappeared into the night.

Chapter Thirteen

The news traveled fast, and by noon everyone in town had heard. Sometime between midnight and dawn, Mary Gast hanged herself in her garage. She threw an extension cord around a rafter, tied a crude noose, slipped it around her neck and kicked aside the three legged stool on which she had been standing.

She didn't make it to morning mass, so that's why people figured she had to be dead by then, but it wasn't until well-after sunset the next day that Chuck, her husband, discovered her body. It was when he got back from the shop, and he searched the whole house but couldn't find a trace. She never went anywhere except to church—she never even went to the grocery store—he did all the shopping. He could never explain why, but he decided finally to check the garage.

By then the sub-zero weather had frozen her body solid. Her eyes had turned to yellowish icicles that had dripped out of their sockets and frozen to her cobweb gray cheeks. A single dirty brown light bulb cast its dingy glow along the outline of her face; it caught the white curve of her neck, lit up her hair and fell over the electrical cord, tracing it until it disappeared into the blackness above. She dangled there above the cracked, grease-stained floor another three hours as they waited for Elmo Voivode to get back from Seneca and file a report.

It was Elmo who cut her down. Two volunteer firemen helped him ease the body into a burlap shroud. It was another half hour before the ambulance took her away.

The funeral was a small one; Mary had a sister somewhere, but no one knew how to reach her, and Chuck's brother in Fargo was too sick to travel. Father Misere's homily was brief. He tried to make a connection between her death and the fact that it was Valentine's Day, but the somewhat perverse and mystifying analogy seemed only to draw attention to the one word he was trying to avoid. The usual funeral dinner was not held, and by noon she was in the ground, the handful of mourners that had gathered about the grave was dispersed, and Wirt was left to lower the body into the earth. He felt bad because he had to hold off the funeral for a week – it took him that long to get the ground unthawed, and his crew was working overtime as it was. There had been a record number of deaths lately and he couldn't keep up. He was thinking about getting another machine to avoid a similar embarrassment in the future.

It was Saturday, and Chuck stayed home the rest of the day, but Monday morning he was back at work up at Kern's. He spent the day replacing a set of rings in a five-sixty, ate supper in the café, then went home.

It felt strange to be alone. He sat at the side window and looked out at the woods behind the house. The February wind rustled icily through the blood-black branches. They moaned piteously in the night, a gnarled, warped and tangled mass, and as they scraped against one another he listened, intent on the dark lullaby until he fell asleep against the sill and slept there until dawn.

For the next couple months he kept up the same routine, but then, when spring broke and the snows receded and the ice started losing its hold on the land once again, his work began to fall off up at the shop. He slowed way down, he seemed confused, and he made mistakes. Dell, without telling Arly, always made it a point now to keep an eye on

Chuck's work but he could do only so much. One day, Chuck sent Will Irons home with his 706 after replacing a gear in the transmission, but he hadn't recalibrated the gears correctly. Will made it about two miles down the road. The gear box simply disintegrated.

The long walk back to town gave Will plenty of time to work himself into a state of absolute rage. He was one of the biggest farmers around and the last thing Arly wanted was to lose him as a customer, so he tore up the bill, sent him home with another 706 off the lot, and headed back into the shop for a talk with Chuck.

"I'm afraid – gonna have—let you go, Chuck."

The old mechanic was working on an alternator, replacing the brushes. He set his screwdriver down on the bench and stared through the grimy shop window. The window was tinged blue with smoke and dust. Dust was also banked up on the sill, littered with insect carcasses. He seemed more intent on studying the carcasses and the fly specks on the glass than in listening to what Arly was saying. The sharp spring breeze that cut through one of the cracked panes breasted out the spider webs there like billowing sails.

"I don't want to. But—Just not workin' out anymore. So. Let's just—there's nothin'—talk about. Irons—he's. Well. Lotta damage there. Store'll pay for it. I'll do that. Won't take it out—your wages, But gotta do—that's it. That's just it, that's all." He waved his hand past his face and hurried off. Then before closing the shop door behind him, he added charitably over his shoulder. "They're hiring up to Gibbet's—Seneca."

Chuck didn't see the point in going all the way up there for that. He calculated mentally. Social security in two years. What's the point? Old enough. He picked out the tools that were his—he bought a few over the years, not many, but a few, and went home for the last time.

He started drinking quite a bit then, but people understood easily enough. They thought he should have gone to Gibbets—they were taking on a lot of men his age—but there was no use talking to him about it. He didn't seem to care to do much at all anymore. The weeds grew higher and higher around his house. All summer his old '52 Chevy sat in the driveway with a flat tire and the hood up, a trouble light dangling there. It didn't matter. The only place he ever went was up to the post office in the morning, then to the corner table by the window in the café for a couple eggs and some toast, then across to the bar for a bottle of something or other, and then home again.

When winter came he eliminated the café from his rounds, stopped at the bar every other day, buying two bottles instead of one, and gave up on the post office altogether. The snow filled in around his Chevy and completely blocked off the front door to the house. He could still get in and out through the back door though—he was able to keep a little goat path for himself open there—but the snow was so high in the driveway that Ollie Leaper couldn't even get his fuel oil truck in close enough to the house anymore to refill the tank for the furnace. Chuck just waved him off, nodding his head slowly back and forth as he stood on the back stoop, clutching the collar of his thin linen coat close around his neck. Ollie started walking up to him to talk, but Chuck disappeared back in the house, so he left. He wasn't worried—he knew Chuck had a wood burning stove in the kitchen, and he never heated the upstairs. He got his fuel from the grove, and from the looks of it he'd been back and forth quite a few times already.

In fact, as the winter wore on and the icy winds encased the town deeper and deeper into an especially bitter cold year, about the only time people saw him anymore was when he was out in the woods. Driving past, they'd catch a glimpse of him gathering the dead limbs and hauling them back by the armful to his house. Or they'd see him sawing away at the lower limbs, his thin black coat billowing out around him like the wings of an enormous bird.

At night then, he'd be there at the side window, a vague silhouette in the dingy light. It was as if he'd always been there, so permanent a fixture he'd become. He listened to the wood in the stove, crackling away, cries rising from the twisted roots of the grove. He gazed out at the blood-black branches weaving themselves through the stars above, one darkness knit to another.

Chapter Fourteen

Will Kern stood at the parts counter, leafing through a sheaf of yellow pages. His cigarette had turned to a cylinder of ash where he set it on the counter edge, burning a black scar into the wood. There was any number of such scars all along the counter. He flicked the still burning butt to the cement floor, crushed it under his boot, tapped out another Old Gold from the pack in his shirt pocket and touched a match to the tip, all without taking his eyes off the page of numbers in front of him.

Jim was working up by the window, putting away an order of plow shares on the rack there. The rack stretched from floor to ceiling displaying row after row of razor-sharp iron blades. He checked off the number stamped into each blade on a page from the same yellow form his uncle was using.

It was a still early autumn morning. Though every once in a while a breeze would catch in the stand of poplars across the street, their leaves flickering like bright yellow fish, the slight stirring in the branches seemed only to accentuate the calm. Dell's hammer in the shop, Grandma Kern working at the adding machine on the desk in the office, tapping at the keys, drawing back the black handle on the side, scratching down the numbers in her enormous black ledger—all established their rhythms within the stillness and became part of it.

Another gust washed over the leaves and as Jim glanced out at them he noticed Junky John inching his way through the weeds in front of the store. A crumbling sidewalk meandered there, and he followed it with precise, measured steps, a salivic stub of a cigar stuck between his lips. Beneath the ragged rim of an antique sailor's cap, tiny gray eyes peered out through thick blasts of cigar smoke. The eyes were set in a round face of black bristles, and thick black hairs also grew in profusion from his ears and from the flattened stub of his nose. His coat collar was buttoned tightly to the chin. Every season he wore the same coat—a torn, greasy rag, stained with everything he had ever come in contact with for the last hundred years.

He lived in a yellow two room shack just north of the store. He kept a dozen pekingese on the property, sequestered there by two rows of snow fences that strung a rickety semi-parallel course between the house and the garage. All around the garage stood the carcasses of rusting automobiles, cannibalized and riddled with bullet holes. The holes, as well as the shimmering pools of shattered windshields in the weeds, indicated the Sabbath afternoon pursuits of bored farmboys.

Jim kept an eye on his progress through the weeds, then as he hefted an especially long share over his head and slid it into place, the screen door opened and slammed shut. A flurry of flies rose in its wake.

John stood in a pool of sunlight, taking a slow survey of all the shelves and the bins that surrounded him. He looked up at the young Kern who was still perched on the ladder. He extracted his cigar, tipped the ash to the floor, then raised the cigar in a type of salute to the boy.

"Help you, John?" Will called from the counter.

"No, sir. Well, yes sir. You might…"

"What d'ya need?"

"Well, what I need is…What I need is…" And as he trailed off a second time his face took on a sudden ashen glow, and his gray eyes fixed on a line of saws against the far wall. "What I need, looks…you got right here."

He ran his thumb across each serried edge, then he tested the feel of the handles, lavishing a precise study of the most minute details until, satisfied that he had found the best of the lot, he headed up to the counter to pay.

"That all you need then, the saw?" Will asked.

"Yeah that…Well…No…come to…think…" He wandered off to the middle of the store and paused by the scale on the nail counter. He eyed the thick glass platter on the scale and the counterweights stacked beside it, then ran his finger up and down up and down the series of baroque balance arms. "No…No…" He muttered under his breath. "No…No…I'll need…I'll need a ladder."

"Got one right there by the paint. See there?" Will pointed with his cigarette.

"By the paint. Yes…By the paint. Of course. By the paint. Here it is, by the paint."

He inspected every step and every hinge, then he climbed up the first few steps, testing them with his weight. "Have…to do…Guess. Better 'n…"

He dragged the ladder up to the counter.

Will wrote out the sales slip. "Nineteen ninety nine."

John shook his head slowly, considering, then he extracted a blackened leather wallet from somewhere deep inside his coat. He drew two tens from the tangle of bills nesting there.

"You know," Will said, "been tellin' you—You oughta put some of that cash in the bank."

"For what? Banks shit on you, then piss on you! Then shit on you again! That's what banks do!"

He dropped his penny change into his pocket.

On the way out, he glanced up at Jim again from the corner of his eye, was about to say something, but decided otherwise and left.

The deep morning silence returned, through which Grandma Kern tapped out another series of numbers on the adding machine. The strain of the black wooden handle, The keys snapping against the ribbon: sequestered behind the office walls she worked away unseen; the same again as Dell back in the shop, making his presence known only by an occasional hammer blow, or the whirring of an air wrench.

Will and Jim continued putting away the parts shipment, dispensing the greasy boxes to their appropriate bins. The wind was picking up a bit outside, lifting the screen door open, letting it fall softly again against the frame, the poplars bending a bit deeper to the breeze, but otherwise everything continued to drift along its ancient patterned course.

From outside came the sound of a saw biting through something metal. Will took note of it, though only with a single raised eyebrow, then went back to work writing out numbers on little wire tags. After a few more minutes, however, his curiosity grew stronger; he put down his pen, lit another cigarette and headed outside.

Junky John was standing on the top step of his new ladder, and with his new saw was cutting off the edge of the store roof. Will didn't say anything right away and John, intent on his labor, didn't notice the audience gathering beneath him—Jim had meanwhile joined his uncle and was staring up, like him, as if they were witnessing the arrival of some bizarre messiah from the heavens engaged in some inscrutable symbolic gesture.

"John," Will finally managed. "What are you doing?"

He extracted the saw from the deepening cut, examined the edge of the blade, then, satisfied, set the saw back in motion. "Cuttin' off the roof here."

"I see that. I see that, John."

The sawing continued. A scrap of the gutter fell off and landed softly in the weeds.

"So, John. You mind tellin' me why?"

"Your bildung's goin' out too far." He used his saw to point north to his house, and as he inscribed an arc in the air with his blade he said, "This here's my territory. I measured. You're near a foot over."

He set the saw back in its deepening groove.

"I didn't know that, John."

"Now you do."

"Well, you know, we need that roof."

"Not sayin' you don't." He stopped sawing. "But I need what's mine." The saw went back to work.

"Maybe we could compromise."

"No. I don't think so." A scrap of asphalt joined the shorn gutter below.

"This is damage, John."

"It's all damage."

"You can't just…"

"I'm doin' it."

"John, this is no good. This won't do."

The saw flew out of its cut. "Don't you…No one!" And he stood there, transfixed: two cindery eyes staring down, the sun glinting off his blade. But he had no further words to offer. He descended slowly, lowering his blade to his side as he came, then draggled home through the weeds, leaving the ladder behind.

From the boards of his rotting stoop he turned and gazed out over the sea of pigeon weed that separated his house from the store. The wind was growing stronger by the minute now; it washed through the knotty green-gray stand in violent whirls and eddies, and it wasn't long before the sky itself came to match the color of the weeds. The sun disappeared for the last time behind the thickening curtain of storm clouds and the first rolls of thunder ground across the blackened heavens.

Will and Jim had gone back inside soon after Junky John left, and there was no one else to be seen anywhere on the street. He stood, gazing back at his work on the roof as the storm gathered around him. The first great splotches of rain started to fall, striking his face, stinging it. Autumn was on its way. Storms came up fast now. Out of nowhere. Right out of nowhere.

His dogs scurried away for shelter through the hole in the garage. Every once in a while a nose poked out, sniffing at the air, and a nervous paw ventured forth to test the rising mud, but otherwise the thunder kept them at bay.

Finally, the rain pouring off his hat and his coat completely drenched, John tossed the watery stub of his cigar to the mud and went inside.

Will had been watching him through one of the tiny windows in the back of the parts bins. "He finally went in."

"What?" Jim asked, coming back into the narrow bin to join him.

"John. He finally went in out of the rain. I've seen him out in the snow like that too. In the middle of a blizzard."

"Is he coming back to finish the roof?"

Will smiled. "No. No, he won't be back." He crushed his cigarette under his boot. "I'll leave the ladder there just in case though."

They both went out to the parts counter and stared into the rain.

The storm washed over the town and beat against the window panes. Grandma Kern emerged from the office to join them.

"Feel sorry for him I suppose," she said. Will had already told her the story.

"Yeah, not much of a life."

"No."

The three of them gazed into the rain a while longer.

"You know, they say he's got more degrees than a thermometer," Grandma Kern said.

"Yeah."

"I don't believe it."

"I don't know. Hard to say."

"Well, I don't believe it. What's he doing here then if he's so smart?"

"Not every one lives here has to be dumb as a post."

"That's not what I mean. You know what I mean."

"Well, it doesn't matter what a person knows or doesn't know."

"One day he's gonna hurt somebody..."

"He ain't gonna hurt anyone."

"All right then..."

She waved a dismissive hand past her face and disappeared back inside the office. Soon she was adding up her rows of figures again, marking down the tallies in her enormous black ledger.

The rain continued for the rest of the day and on into the night. Autumn was setting in fast. There were frost warnings out already. Soon the town was little more than a dozen or so yellow patches of light framed by the icy darkness, the dim light in Junky John's shack simply joining all the others.

Chapter Fifteen

In the sky above Isaac Johnson's lot hovered a black speck. Autumn clouds unfurled about it like ashen sheets, and the wind from which it seemed suspended tugged it obtusely so that it dipped, caught, and dipped again, scribbling out its cabalistic message against the dim shroud of the setting sun.

Jim was coming back from the store. Wind tore through all the weeds and scattered garbage everywhere along the street where he walked. For two years now since the sixth grade, he went up to the store to work after school. Before, he was expected to be there only on Saturdays, but his father figured he was old enough now to put some time in every day.

The wind cut and winnowed its way across the stubble field in the middle of town. The black speck was there now, rising higher and higher, becoming harder and harder to track as it faded in and out of sight. Finally, it disappeared altogether, absorbed completely into the cloud banks.

"Kern!" It was Cut Schnuller calling to him. Jim could just barely make him out from between the trunks of two charred oaks on Johnson's lot. The grizzly old man motioned toward him with his free hand—the crippled one. "This'll hold you for awhile!" He pointed at the sky.

One foot resting against a rusted strap on Johnson's saw wheel, two enormous balls of baler twine at his feet, he fed the twine out through his good hand and continued beckoning.

"Come here, boy! This'll keep you busy all right! Look what I got for you here now!"

Jim came up to him. With his eyes he followed the twine from the ground to the point where it disappeared in the sky, then back again.

"Look at that now! Can't even see what we're seein' anymore!" Cut's hand, which was shorn of three fingers and its thumb, wormed its surviving index finger excitedly at the clouds. "Well, it might be there, it might not. Hard to tell at this point. Hard to tell. Can't even tell you what it looks like any more. Big though! Damn big! Tell you that. Reel it back in here again, see what you see. That's all I can say at this point. That's all I know. Hell! I don't even know that. No sir! *I don't even know that!* That's a fact! Only seen it once, and I thought to myself…Oh hell now, hell now, hell now…Oh, there it is, Yeah feel it tuggin! Feel it tuggin again! Fella can have all sorts of fun with one of these! You just let her go! Yup! Come on now. You give it a try here!"

He thrust the twine into Jim's hands.

"Careful now! Light as you are, it's liable to take you right outa here!"

Jim felt the tug of the rope, surprised at how powerful it was.

"Don't hold it back—just keep feedin' it. That's all it wants now anyway!"

The rope disappeared up into the clouds, and the more he fed through his fingers the heavier it became. He tried holding it back, but it was no use.

"Well, I gotta get goin', so she's all yours now." With the one protruding digit of his severed hand he made a grab at Jim's nose, then with playful triumph raised his fin—like stump in the air. "I gotcha!" he joked. "Gotcha by the nose!"

He wandered off through the weeds to his tiny blue camping trailer tucked away in the trees on the edge of the lot. There was more rust on the trailer than paint and the bottom half was covered with moldering plywood turned black with age, but it's where he lived summer and winter. In the summer he'd sit out front all day, sometimes alone, sometimes with his cronies, Coke, Junky John and Chief; but in the winter the only trace of him would be the thin trail of smoke from his chimney pipe. Instead of groundhog day, the joke was, they had Cut Schnuller day. If Cut came out and didn't see his shadow there'd be six more weeks of drinking.

A mangy black poodle jumped up from where it had been playing in the stubble field and went chasing after him. It circled around the old man, snapping and snarling all the time, then ran up to the sill of the trailer door, sniffing it and wagging its tail as its master approached from behind, then the two if them disappeared inside.

Jim continued feeding out the line, letting himself get lost imagining what was on the other end, but simultaneously feeling awkward and conspicuous out there all alone, he considered, almost immediately, simply walking away from the whole thing, and the more line he fed out, the more he felt like leaving.

He imagined Cut inside, laughing at him. What else would he be doing? It was some sort of game he was playing. But then his fascination would grow again as the sky greedily took up foot after foot of his line with unceasing appetite. It slipped easily through his fingers and it seemed like it could go on and on and on, but soon the clouds and their ashen curtains would devour everything he had, and then what? There would be nothing left, and then what? He would have to let go then. He looked down at his store of line—that would be a long time yet, but still…

The sky grew darker and darker. He could see the yellow light in the window glowing faintly from Cut's trailer. Cut moving around inside. The pictures plastered to all the walls. Grimy magazines everywhere piled up. The black stench of his breath came back to him as Jim stood there, and the memory made him close his eyes in disgust.

Rotted gums, three remaining teeth in his mouth—that was him. He was always there. He would always be there…

He turned away and cast his eyes skyward, letting his gaze slip out of focus, grow hazy, blur in the uniform mistiness of empty space. He loved to gaze into the sky for the sake of its undivided unmeasurableness, like the land itself that reached out all around him in an unbroken void.

He wanted to rush home and write. He would write about this. A poem. He would send it to his brother. Would he like it?

Then he thought again. No, it was better for now just to stand there, absorbed in this perfect void; then shifting his focus he became aware of a figure crossing the darkening horizon. Barely visible through a break in the groves north of town, the figure advanced one slow inch at a time, pulled along by an enormous walking stick. It was Coke embarked on his usual rounds. He was out there almost every night at this time, circling the town, then his circuit completed, he would take up his post at Nob's hovering in some shadowy corner until closing time.

There was no longer any color in the trees, fields, or sky: the autumn was long past its prime and the once vibrant reds and golds had long ago been stripped from the now black branches; all the surrounding fields had been plowed into black, except for the half acre of stubble in the middle of town but Digger White—it was his land—would be taking care of that any day, and the sky itself rarely showed even the faintest trace of blue anymore, it revealed only one level of gray on top of another. This is the way it would be now month after month, but at the same time that he dreaded the cold and the darkness, he also looked forward to it. There was a type of sadness to it all that made him feel uniquely alive: it was an equally beautiful and forbidden feeling, one of loneliness that cut him off from everything and everyone, but that allowed him the chance to see things and to hear things that he knew instinctively were lost on the crude, foolish and thoughtless people that surrounded him.

It helped explain his affinity for morbid outsiders like Coke and Cut and all the others hidden away in the musty, dank corners of town. It also helped explain his fear of them—their secret insect movements, their occasional migrations from one abandoned building to another, or from one shack to another. The attraction and repulsion came to him in equal parts, and suspended between these two poles he worked secretly in his mind to puzzle out the riddle: how could he swear simultaneous allegiance to two such opposite forces?

It was the same riddle woven into the line feeding itself out now into the dark. He was almost unconscious of its movement, so steady had it become, but as it slipped through his fingers the wind stung his face with a fine mist growing colder and colder as if it would drive him away from the lot once and for all. It was pointless, and he knew he could only abandon the absurd task. There would be no end to it. It would go on and on forever and ever.

The sky above was more black than gray and soon the siren would blow. He thought for a moment—he could invent some ingenious method of hauling the line back in—loop it around the saw wheel frame for leverage maybe and keep tying it off— but dark as it was and cold as it was he soon abandoned all hope in this direction.

Pulling heaven down to earth would have to wait. He let the line go. It slipped freely from his fingers and was soon charting its own destiny, the line unraveling faster and faster until the ball of twine itself skated away, caught fast in some brambles, dislodged itself, then, grown considerably lighter, flew off into the night sky.

The darkness gathered it greedily up, as if it had been waiting all this time for the right opportunity to snatch back a misplaced item—some comet fallen out of place, he thought following after it with his eyes. He pretended he could keep track of it longer than he actually could, but the only purpose his pretense served was to deepen the strange sense of remorse he felt.

He sat down in the weeds and leaned against the saw wheel. The sky was completely black now without stars or moon. The siren blew, sending the dogs out into the street. The wind itself too seemed to howl all the louder.

To the side he was aware of the light in Cut's window, but he was still intent only on the lightless night sky itself. He no longer felt like writing about it—that feeling had passed—but he needed to sit there and think, and as his thoughts led him further and further away, and as the siren wound down, returning the town again to its evening silence, he began to feel how perfectly at peace he was so long as he remained there, hidden away from everything and everyone. He could see lights other than Cut's from where he sat, and he felt that by simply looking through those windows he could see all the lives inside—what *they* felt, what *they* thought—and all he had to do was look at them.

Driven away. Cut off. He looked out over the town; a handful of lights, and then nothing. The nothingness only inches away. One nothingness bordering another. Between his feelings of pity and disgust the only refuge was an intense numbness, and he sought its safety now as he got up from his spot in the weeds and headed home.

Chapter Sixteen

"Ain't nobody here? Where...Come on! Goin' fishin'! C'mon..."

"Daddy, Don't..."

"Get off that! Le'me be! Hey! Where—everybody?"

Draggling behind her drunk husband, horrified by the lurching violence in each of his steps, Betty Sedler continued pleading as they headed up the walk to their daughter's house. His insane antics these last few months had worn deep lines into her face, and unable to eat for weeks now, her long-suffering reduced her to little more than a skeleton figure tracking him in an absurd attempt to draw him back to the provinces of reason.

"Daddy, you can't..."

"Ain't nobody gonna tell me nothin', least of all you, woman!" His fist shook abstractly at the sky, then he almost sent himself crashing to the sidewalk as he attempted to turn around in mid-curse and launch another slurred volley. His words fell short and broken, "Leave 'lone...Town fulla...Devils, junkyards..."

The tally so far for his latest binge was around fifty thousand dollars—all money out of their retirement savings gone to buy invisible herds of apaloosas and a broken down farm to run them on. It was the same almost every summer. He'd buy everything he could or couldn't get his hands on, and as soon as word got out that George Sedler was writing checks again, every crook in the county had a deal for him. They knew just how to play him too—treat him like a king and rob him blind. But every good thing has to come to an end. George Sedler's summer was long over now, and after this last escapade there wasn't anything left to take. Of course he was still writing checks, but there was no longer any money left to cover them.

"Yes sir! Got three grandson's! Triple K! Triple K ranch! That's a fact!"

The drama was being enacted midway between their car—its doors swung wide open, parked at the kind of novel angle only a professional drunk can manage—and the house, the front window of which Nora's face now appeared. Above them bare limbs of the oak tree swayed menacingly in the wind. A storm was coming, clearly prophesized by the whisping clouds far above the oak—mare's tails, and not far behind them, deep black plumes rising from the horizon.

"Goddamned junkyards chokin' me off! Killin' me! Killin' all of us..." his arms flailing like sails broken lose, flying madly from the topmast as he tries to aim himself back to the sidewalk, only to be thrown off course repeatedly: the captain was drunk and the ship, floundering.

Betty wept; on her knees now, hands clenched in prayer to this strange, whirling devil that was her husband, the wind coming up, the sky darkening, a flash of lightning cut over the grove.

"Ain't nobody gonna tell me nothin'! Goddamned crooks runnin' the whole show when folks like me and my dad—built this place, built up this whole country here! Money changers in the temple! that's what they are! Money changers in the temple!"

Nora appeared on the front steps. Betty looked up from where she knelt in the grass, one skeleton hand wringing another. "It's terrible! Terrible! He disappeared this morning and went downtown, so he's been in the bar I don't know how long. Finally someone from up there called me and said I'd better come do something. Do something! What! What can I do! Look at him! Well by the time I got down there..."

"A cabal of sinners! Poison! They put poison—the water! Poison in the land!" He shook his fists at the sky.

By this time Arly finally pried himself out of his chair and joined Nora on the steps.

"What...Come on now! Cryin' out loud! Get him in the house! Now!" The direct order was issued to his mother in law, but she only shook her head.

"I've been trying to, Arly. You try talking to him!"

"I don't care! I want him out of the yard!"

"He's drunk! There's no talking to him!"

A black lump curled off Arly's tongue in a gelatinous tobacco drizzle that pooled by the rose bush at his feet. He bared his teeth for another attack.

"Damnit George! Get in the house, now!"

George spun around, his hair like white flames in the wind, his gray-blue eyes leering woundedly at his son-in-law.

"Arly! Aha...By God! It was your dad and my dad what built up this land! Arm in arm, they were like brothers! Come out here and made this place with their bare hands! Now look at it! People dyin' of cancer! Can't even breath the air! Poison!"

"I don't care about none of that, George! Get in the..."

"Yeahp! Your dad and my dad, come out here—honest men! Good men! Dug and clawed at the earth with their bare hands and made it grow! *They made it grow!* Now we got nothin' but greed chokin' us off! Mark my word! Mark my word all of you! We're gonna pay for it! We're gonna pay for all of it! But I'm gonna change that! I'm gonna build paradise! Put up the Ten Commandments on all the hills so people drivin' by 'll know! They'll know what's what!"

"That farm he bought...Imagine that, buying a farm—eighty years old and buying a farm!" Betty stared blankly at the gray clouds gathering in the sky. "Fifty thousand dollars gone—and it still isn't paid for—he's going to lose it all too, all of it! How's he going to take care of it! And every time I turn around, he's buying another herd of horses or another car! And we had it so good for so many years! What do we have to live on now?"

"Damnit George, get in the house! Now! Everyone in the county can hear you!"

"And they're *gonna* hear me too! The gospel according to George Sedler! The Ten Commandments on every hill! Don't think I'm foolin' neither! People are gonna know! Got too many sinners runnin' this show and they're gonna burn in hell—I'm gonna see to it!"

Arly snaped his fist shut in the air as if catching a fly. "Don't go talkin' crazy George."

"Don't tell me—don't tell me what I don't know!"

Arly half turned to Nora, "Just do something about him! I'm tired of this all the time!" Then, punctuating his authority with a righteously indignant grunt, he stomped away inside the house. Alone in the kitchen he poured a glass of whiskey, drank it off, waited for his orders to be carried out, and fumed.

It started to really get bad about three years ago when George dropped twenty thousand to build a show barn in Weed for rodeos, only there weren't any rodeos and now it just stood there, a hundred thousand square foot liability. Then all the horses and the cars—the money they saved for retirement—nothing left. "And I'll end up buyin' their groceries!" He mumbled aloud to himself as he poured another glass.

The phone rang.

"Hello, Mayor Kern."

His voice brightened. "Hi, Kiddo!"

"How're things in your neck of the woods?" She laughed.

"Don't know—gonna make it tonight."

"What?"

"Up to—bar. Don't know."

"Nora?"

"Father in law—drunk out here. Imagine I'm gonna have—take him back to Weed. Grandma's with him, but she don't drive."

"So he drove all the way from Weed?"

"Yeah. Don't know how—made it. Pretty bad shape. If—do get it up there—be around dark."

"I'll be there. Got nothin' out here. Bob's been down in Hunger all day. I imagine he's passed out in Bernie's back room by now."

"I—better go. See ya."

He hung up and finished his glass. He felt his thoughts starting to clear so he went to work charting his course for the night. He could still hear George outside. He poured another glass. Drive grandma back in the pickup. Nora can take *him*. Damn fool drunk. Don't even want to *see* him. Cause enough trouble.

Betty was still weeping as she and her daughter entered through the porch. The older Sedler's once erect posture had collapsed, so she was little more than a bizarre, piteous beggar woman come calling, sheltered momentarily by an almsgiver arm. Nora's black hair was falling down around her face; she had taken off her coat and draped it around her mother's shoulders, and as she bent closer to adjust the coat, her hair became completely unpinned. Its black shroud fell thickly over both faces.

Arly swirled his glass surreptitiously under the tap in the sink. "He still out there?"

"Yes," Betty answered. "Just sitting there in the car. What am I supposed to do with him, Arly? Everything's ruined…just gone—gone, gone, gone gone." She waved her hand meekly in the air like a child. "Sometimes all I want to do is just die."

"Better get back him back before dark. Storm comin'."

"We had it so good—our house, plenty of money—he had his couple of horses he kept out in the barn, and then he starts buying all this land because he thinks he can go out and start all over again or something—oh he's got plans all right, big plans—ski resorts, race tracks, you name it. And then when they get him talking up at the bar—and he loves to talk—I think he's losing his mind—well, they get him talking up there and he just gets madder and madder—especially about the junkyards and how when Christ comes back he's going to strike everyone in town dead with a bolt of lightning, and how…"

"Okay, that's enough! Don't want—hear anymore about it! Let's just get him home—be done with this."

At his bedroom window, Jim saw and heard most everything—from his grandfather's brimstone oration to his father's final say in the matter. He looked at his grandfather sitting in the car now: a violently metamorphosed figure, strangely and instantly heroic in Jim's mind; after all, the outlandish drama the old man had just produced brought life to the dead world—the kind of life his father was trying desperately to extinguish.

And as Jim sat there considering the strangeness of the events unfolding before him, he realized that what he was witnessing was the behavior his parents were trying, in their own crude way, to shield from him. It was all something secret and shameful to them, but as this thought crystallized and one set of questions finally found their answer, the answer to another set of questions which he was beginning to ask himself remained completely beyond his grasp, though only moments ago he overheard his father give the answer clearly and distinctly. For now, it was enough to sit there and contemplate his grandfather in his magnificently drunken state, resting between acts.

Jim sneaked outside, and as his nervous steps drew him closer to the indecipherable slurry of his Grandfather's words that came pouring forth, the oak tree above shuddered blackly with increasing violence, gnarled limbs weathering yet another storm wind mixed with a dry, cackling laugh from below: the old king continued honing his epithets with mad gesticulations at the steering wheel and the rear-view mirror, his hands like a rain of granite slabs pounding away in merciless punctuations at the already battered interior.

"By God, there's the old cowboy himself!" He shouted as his grandson came up and peered in at him through the open window. With as much dexterity as his drunken state could marshall he went to work prying himself out of the car, but the door was jammed somehow, and as he beat his doubled fists against it he accompanied his labors with a litany of curses.

"Godamn....Godamned door here! Damn latch! Goddamned... Goddamned door here..." Finally, the door relented and he fumbled himself out onto the lawn. Once he got his bearings again he raised himself to his full height; and as he stood there, towering above the boy, sputtering and laughing, enormous drops of rain exploded into the dust around them like spidery meteors.

"Yeah, I tell ya! Your old grandpa, sure pulled one over 'em this time! Quite a guy, ain't he? I tell you what, yes sir! I tell you what! They're gonna know a thing or two! Your grandma—that old woman...Why I got girlfriends all around the state here—don't need her tellin' me what's what! I got cowgirls here to Sisseton drop their drawers for me any time I say! Don't tell me what I *can* do, what I *can't* do!"

Lightning rolled out above them in dull yellow blooms. Though rain still fell only in splotches here and there, it wouldn't be long before the full storm let loose.

"Look at all the things I'm doin' here! Buildin'—empire! Got a herd of hundred appaloosa comin' in—Montana! Got deals goin' here to—why I got deals goin' way up—Manitoba! I'm talkin' to 'em! Talkin' to everyone knows anything 'cause they know me—everybody knows anything knows me! George Sedler! Yes sir! I'm a Sedler! Here to Settle! Yes sir! I'm the settlin' man 'cause I know how to deal! Been dealin' this an' that all my life so don't tell me what's what 'cause I got it all figured out—million dollars, goddamned junkyard graveyard sons of bitches rob me goddamned them—stole my gates! Goddamned them! And they're gonna pay for it too! Every last damn sinner in the whole damn county! It's right there! It's right there in the Bible—don't tell me it ain't there! Don't tell me what I don't know! Had that Dan Patch beat every automobile in the county! You know all about that though—told you all about that—now—gonna take you out—introduce you—my girlfriends—take you all around here! They wanta meet you! Told 'em all about you! Yeah, gonna take you around show you a thing or two—show you what this country's gonna be! Ten Commandments on every hill! George Sedler, that's your grandpa! He's gonna be in charge from now on! Don't tell me ***nothin'***!"

Thunder tore the sky and the fury of the storm rained down upon them; Jim dove into the car for shelter, his grandfather after him, his voice still roaring as he pulled the door shut. "By God! She gonna rain all right! She gonna rain and rain and rain! Wash every last junkyard off the face of the earth! Eddie Deer! Worst junkman there is—goes off—buys a church—gonna invite—Pope—say the mass in Latin! Stinkin' up the air so bad, can't even breathe! Got junkyards everywhere you look—one after another—and him—invitin' the Pope! Flies off—why—good God! Flies off—Devil's Lake every Sunday—'cause they say it—Latin up there! Then all he's got is junkyard after junkyard stinkin' up the air! Stinkin' up the whole county! Why, when I was a boy, Weed was gonna be somethin'! My dad—he worked in the bank twenty years—good man—buildin' up—town—then you got these outlaws come in—you know what?"

He snatched up Jim's hand in his gnarly fist, leaned his head down, then pressed two of the boy's captive fingers against the back of his skull. "There, feel that? Feel that bump! Jesse James give me that! Yes he did! Come in—held up the bank when I was with my Dad one day—I was there all right! Yes I was—tell you the kind of guy I was—hit me with his gun on the way out! I went after him but he was too fast for me—he was on his horse and gone before I even got out on the street! Now they got these jokers come out here—throw me down the well—break my arm! Then they steal my gates on top of it..."

For a few moments the roar of his voice was finally outmatched by the thunder and the rain. But refusing to admit defeat, he tore on, battling through with a completely unintelligible tirade—one storm striving to be heard above another in an impossible contest until he managed, with nothing but sheer stubbornness on his side, to outshout the black weather; meanwhile, the crushed fingers of his recently released hand playing hopefully at the door latch, Jim stared into a bleary windshield.

"No sir! Nobody's gonna tell *me* what's what by God! I built this land! I made this land what it is! I got—all figured out! Yes sir, I got—all figured out—I tell you what—I tell you what it's gonna be—gonna leave all of you something to be proud of! Each one of you boys gets a farm—that's God's plan that's what it is! Set each one of you up with a hundred cattle and a hundred horses and a hundred this and a hundred that! Just like *my* father did for me, and he was a great man, my father. He was a wise man. He wrote me letters you know, and I still got 'em—every single one of 'em. He was a great man all right, and he was a wise man, and they killed him just like that! By God, by God, by God..."

The struggle to make himself heard through the storm finally took its toll. His massive head drooped to his chest and his arms fell limp, but just as suddenly as the wind left his own sails, the storm outside blew itself out. With one final falling crash of thunder, the rain dropped off to a trickle as the old man could only murmur, "Lord...Mercy...Christ...Lord...Mercy..." An abbreviated kyrie itself trailing off as the sky cleared and the birds started singing once again. The sea and the wind had gone to war—each defeating each.

The old man slept and was instantly dreaming.

Arly shot out of the house. He pulled his hat down tight and yelled back through the porch screen. "C'mon, before—picks up again!"

He yanked the car door open, peered in at Jim, then jabbed his thumb over his shoulder. "You get in the house—stay there. You're mother and me, we're takin' em back!"

Jim slid out. Arly shook his father-in-law by the shoulders. "George! Wake up, damnit! Move over here! Nora's gonna take you home! C'mon!" As he spoke he prodded the old man across to the passenger seat, unheedful of the slurred protests and the feeble, still half-dreaming prayers, settling him there, slumped over. He slammed the door and stormed off across the lawn to his pickup in the alley.

No longer weeping, but her eyes red and her hands unsteady, Betty climbed in beside her son-in-law. He turned the key, raced the engine, and, the instant she closed the door, dropped it into gear then tore off through the ruts and the puddles to the main road. Meanwhile, Nora got behind the wheel beside her unconscious father, straightened the car in the driveway again, then backed out to the street.

The caravan headed off to Weed, while in the western sky above, shafts of golden light like mile high pillars of transparent marble cut through the slowly descending curtain of purple clouds.

Arly snapped his Copenhagen tin against the bar top."Sick of—whole thing!"

"Well, you oughta be! You have every right to be!" Anna Lee drained her wine then waved the empty glass to signal another round.

He poked a finger length of snuff in his mouth and worked it into place with his tongue. "No good, what he does."

"It's a shame. And then to make you responsible!"

Neb set the drinks down in front of them. Arly spit out a stream of tobacco juice on the floor, then took a swallow. "Not gonna put up with—any more. That's—fact!"

"But what can you do?"

"Gonna see—lawyer. Get him settled down. Get him blackballed or something. People got no right—take advantage of him, that's all they do!"

"I suppose. He's an old man. Doesn't know what he's doin'."

"No he don't! That's just it! He's—crazy old man. Eighty years—doin' these things.Got no respect for him! He's off limits to the house! Told Nora that. He come over, I want him out!"

"And you have every right too!"

"I know I do! Comes over—two three times a week—brings fish he's caught. I told Nora he don't come over no more! And that's final! He comes in the store, wants to buy something—half a pound of nails, flashlight battery—I don't care what—I'm not sellin'. Final!"

"That's right. It's your store, after all. You can sure say who you *can* deal with and who you *won't*."

"That is a fact. That *is a fact*!"

"He sure got you worked up, don't he?"

"Makes—so damn mad!"

He swallowed the last of his drink and ordered another round.

There was hardly anyone else in the place. John Coke stood in the shadow at the far end of the bar, his hands gnarled around his enormous walking stick. Every once in a while he tapped the stick against the floor in a mournful beat, his empty eye sockets staring off into smoke and vacancy.

In the corner booth, Will Spear and Herman Budd slurred their way through a game of poker. They chuckled to themselves intermittently over some obscene joke they kept going between them as they played. The only other person there was Old Sarah Seher. She was slumped over like a rotten bundle of sticks, her head cradled into her arms on the bar. Every once in a while she'd cough herself awake, order another Grain Belt, complain about the high price, then cast her yellow eyes around the room. But unable once again to pierce the eternal gloom there, she would settle back, defeated, into her arms once again.

Anna Lee crossed her legs and gave the bartop a slap. "You know what, Arly? You've been thinking about this all night now, and it's got you all worked up something terrible. That's not good."

Her playful scolding drew a smile from him. "You're right. Nothing—do about it now."

"No there isn't. Like the man says, Gotta let it go." She took a long swallow of wine. "Sure is a live one in here tonight, ain't it?"

"Yeah. Well, they got the game—softball—over to Madrid tonight."

"Probably got rained out."

"Hard to say. Storm cut a swath pretty much just over here and to the West. We got an inch and a half and Weed got an inch and a quarter. Land up north here didn't get touched but we picked up half an inch last week. Gonna be a good year, I think. Wheat's gonna bring five dollars, easy, and corns been up all along. Beans runnin' good—I bet we get fifty bushels an acre."

"You and your brother always have some darn good crops."

"Yeah, we do. That's Agribusiness, you know. We gotta work seven days a week, that's what we do. Other guys around here, take vacation right in the middle of harvest almost. That's no way to work."

"Now you can't work all the time..." She laughed and winked. "Another round?"

"Yeah. Hey, Neb!"

Neb gave his customary salute.

"I sure like my wine, I guess," she said.

"It's good for you, I hear."

"Feels like it's good for me."

Her car was in the usual place back by the door to the butcher shop.

Chapter Seventeen

Charlie Gaughn's funeral was just getting underway. It was in the heart of the winter now, and as Jim stood on the edge of the ice skating rink in the middle of town he listened as the church bell tolled on. One slow clear and precise note struck over and over, and in the echoing silence between the notes he counted out silently to himself: One, two, three, four, five; one, two, three, four, five…

While he measured out the silence he also kept a running tally of each tolling. In the end it added up to twenty seven. Why twenty seven? Charlie was in his fifties—weren't they supposed to ring it once for every year? Or why not an even number—twenty or thirty, or thirty-three, thirty-three like Christ. If we were all like Christ it should be thirty three. And if Charlie Gaughn isn't Christ than neither am I and none of us are. We die and that's that. Why should there be anything else?

Such associative leaping, though not always so reckless and so transparently flawed, that inevitably concluded in a not always so spiteful an atheism, had become a habit of thinking ever since his stay in the hospital. He was there for over two weeks with pneumonia in both lungs. He'd been out for two months now, but the experience was still clear in his mind.

One morning he simply walked into the living room and collapsed. His knees started shaking, his head was on fire, and it was all he could do to crawl to the sofa, where he laid for the rest of the day in a sweating delirium.

It was impossible to lie still and he was far too weak to sit up, and as he laid there, arms and legs thrashing feebly, his fever unleashed legion upon legion of hellish figures leaping from the abyss—but they were not even figures, simply amorphous identities, or non-identities that appeared on a screen he could not shut out; there seemed no end to them—and there was no end to them. He was pinned there, insect arms and legs quivering, while from out of the constantly metamorphosing shapes arose voices, and the words they spoke appeared to him as visual scripts: the words themselves were visible and just as he could not shut out the invading figures themselves, could not stop their entrances nor predict their exits, neither could he silence their words nor predict what would come next. Audience to his own unveiling self, either awake in his dream or dreaming awake, it was the same because the stage itself did not shift, but what images, what words it contained—that was another matter.

Cars lined the entire length of the sidewalk in front of the church. White sheets of exhaust wound into the cold blue sky. Cars also lined the entire length of the sidewalk all the way down to the new school. A light in the window there glowed darkly behind the gray glass. A black trace of smoke trailed away from the school chimney.

After everyone came back from the graveyard, that's where they'd go—to the gymnasium and the tables that were laid out for them. The funeral hot dish was ready—hamburger, macaroni, corn, and onions mixed together with tomato soup—bubbling away in five gallon vats, unattended: the cooks were also in church with the rest of the mourners, all crowded together into the shivering pews. The choir straining to life now...

He'd been to only a handful of funerals, but enough for him to imagine every detail; more importantly he'd witnessed countless others from the outside—the tolling bell, the row of cars, the half mile procession to Calvary Cemetery west of town, the meal afterwards, the cars driving off. It was all a predictable routine.

His first funeral was his Grandfather's. He remembered the bitter cold and the long sermon but little else other than being bored and somewhat mystified, especially when he saw his uncle Will in tears. Instantly, Jim glanced away as if hit on the head with a club.

Mary Gast's funeral was just as cold, though the sermon wasn't very long at all—at least Father Misere spent more time stammering than speaking as if he either forgot what he was going to say or was just filling in time. Jim didn't understand why his mother brought him along in the first place. She said he had to go and that was that.

The church steeple rose high above the snow banks, and as he gazed up he imagined the enormous iron bell at rest now, the rope dangling all the way to the floor—Charlie Bates clutching it there, ready to pull it back to life.

But at the very top in the bell-chamber itself, the darkness of the seven tiny ever-narrowing rooms stacked beneath and filled with the plaster and marble gloom of stored away statues—stark white faces and chalk hands frozen there—gave way to a shower of light. It poured through locked shutters where pigeons fluttered their wings and cooed soothingly, and it traced the outline of the bell in a soft yellow glow. From the tower the land stretched on endlessly: distance giving away to distance, one nothingness giving away to another.

And flying there, far above, a pilot might notice the town less for its vague geometry than for another of its aspects which had become an almost permanent fixture on the land: the endless procession of funerals. Almost every other week the cars and pickups huddled around the church, a new mound of frozen black dirt waiting on the white snow half a mile west.

Mountains of plowed snow rose up higher than the houses, walling them off from one another so each became an arctic citadel. The snowplows did their work; but they had trouble keeping open even the town's main street and most frequented paths, and the few free passageways all ended in impassable drifts. The wind never stopped blowing either, so roads constantly drifted shut. The town was little more than feeble wisps of chimney smoke, a desolate triangle barely distinguishable from the almost unbroken white plain surrounding it.

The cafe, the bars, the service stations, and, of course, the grocery store were all closed for the day. The implement store was still open though. Jim was on his way there now where he was supposed to help his father clean out the furnace. Arly had been there all morning, working away alone in the office; he didn't like funerals, but he thought it was a good idea for his brother and his mother to go. Both mechanics, Jack and Dell, said they wanted to go as well, and under the circumstances it was impossible to say no, but he let them go with the understanding that both would be putting in extra time tomorrow.

The wind sifted the snow from bank to bank and street to street. Jim stamped his feet on the ice to keep warm. In the snow at his feet someone had tossed a pile of ashes. It was hard to tell what they were doing there—maybe some skaters had built a fire—but that would have been a long time ago. No one used the rink at all anymore since it was put in last November when the town council's plan to provide some wintertime recreation for the emerging leisure class led it, one Saturday afternoon, to haul out the volunteer fire department's two trucks and flood a shored-up section of the lot. That night was quite spectacular—dozens of people crowded the ice, and the council congratulated itself once again. But within two or three days interest dropped off to zero. Then the blizzards started to hit in earnest. The rink sank into oblivion, and it was never mentioned again.

Next to it stood The Depot Club—the original Soo Line depot that had stood beside the tracks south of town since late in the last century. Some out of town couple bought it, moved it and converted it into what was considered, by prevailing standards, an elegant, fine-dining experience. The town wore it as a proud badge of affluence.

The church doors swung open and the pall bearers started down the steps with the casket. They loaded the body into the hearse.

The worms crawl in,
The worms crawl out;

The worms play pinochle

On your snout.

Charlie was dead. There is no doubt whatever about that. He was sick, and then he died. Turned to snuff. Cigarettes. Grandpa Kern. He dead. He dead too. What's the difference? Dead or alive? How can you tell? To live here? This is where people come to die. What else is there to do?

People began to straggle down the steps behind the casket, pulling up their coat collars and adjusting their scarves against the wind and the cold. Wisps of breath and cigarette smoke filled the icy air. Three fantastically fat women were scaling a snowbank on the way to the school—the cooks hurrying to stir the hotdish, get the Jell-O salad out of the refrigerator and attend to the hundred other details to get the mourners fed.

The thoughts that played about in Jim's head as he stood watching on the ice were also products of his time in the hospital. The first two days in his oxygen tent, still delirious, viewing the world through a transparent shroud—its blizzards from atop the hill where the hospital stood, and its nuns with their mysterious ministrations, an occasional priest stopping by to sketch the air at the foot of his bed with a sign of the cross—he felt completely disconnected from everything, but at the same time he felt quite at home and eerily comfortable. When they took the tent away and he was able to navigate brief walks outside his room, the first place he found himself in was the library just down the hall. Its erudite Catholic collection seemed like the living presence, or the real life counterpart of his earlier hallucinations.

"The instinct of imitation is implanted in man from childhood, one difference between him and other animals being that he is the most imitative of living creatures, and through imitation learns his earliest lessons; and no less universal is the pleasure felt in things imitated….A beautiful object, whether it be a living organism or any whole composed of parts, must not

only have an orderly arrangement of parts, but must also be of a certain magnitude; for beauty depends on magnitude and order ... Unity of plot does not, as some persons think, consist in the unity of the hero."

What did it mean to imitate? And the phrase "an orderly arrangement of parts" had in itself an enticing music to it...He let his intuition guide his hand over the shelves, and in his first foray he brought back *Madame Bovary*, *Tess of the D'Urbervilles*, and *Huckleberry Finn* to his bed. The words that appeared to him on the pages cast such a spell that he could not stop reading—he would fall asleep late at night, book in hand, and wake the next morning to find it waiting for him so he could move from his own dreams immediately back into the dream of the book—and the books did seem at first like dreams—how they came to him, what they contained—these deep mysteries that only deepened the more he read. The two weeks seemed like two days, and the unlimited freedom allowed to him by his sick bed was like nothing he'd ever experienced before. It, and the winter outside his window, permitted him the solitude he sought, the profoundest solitude imaginable, touching his heart with a precarious savagery beyond human understanding.

But then he got better and had to come home, where instantly the spell was broken. He tried, but he could no longer concentrate—it was impossible to read even a single page; time began to drag for him like it had never done before, breeding an impatience impossible to deal with: he could not wait until he could hatch from the shell of this old-fashioned German backwater town—and he realized now just how old-fashioned and backwards it was—he was trapped, but when he was away from it he was free, but how was he going to get away? Like Charlie? No.

The silence now was absolute, perfect, a padded soundlessness, like none ever known or perceived anywhere else in the world. It was a primal silence to which he listened as he stood there, his head tilted to the side.

The sky was growing gray. He turned and went off to the store. It was time to go to work.

Arly hadn't left the office all morning, but his own thoughts had managed to take him far beyond the glassed-in domain of dusty, broken-down desks, the massive black safe—its door swung far back on its hinges now in the corner—and the floor to ceiling shelves of tattered, grease-stained shop manuals. The ledger laid open in front of him, but his pencil hadn't entered a single figure in some time. The rusted-out electric heater at his feet pinged and glowed in a feeble red coil, though offered little heat for all its labors, so he still hadn't removed his coat, but kept it zipped to the collar, his hat tilted back on his head. He sat there staring blankly into an unfocused distance, one hand in his coat pocket, the other resting limply across the arm of his chair.

He turned aside and took aim. A mouthful of black juice hit the wastebasket with a metallic splat. He watched it curl down over the crumpled papers there, then pinched off a fresh load and poked it home.

He was out until two the night before with Ana Lee up at Nob's. Things had gotten out of hand. They'd been getting out of hand a lot lately, too.

"C'mon, Mayor! I got the number one spot in your administration right here! Got the number one spot right here..."

People had to know by now. Had to. Be more careful...That's all to...No...Just back out...Back out somehow...Nothing *to* do. Makes me so damn mad. My fault too. Shoulda never let it...

"Goddamned..." Startled by his own voice, he looked around, half-expecting someone to be there in the office with him. But there was no one after all. He shook his head and suddenly shouted to the ceiling, "Goddamned fucking...Goddamned son of a bitch..."

And as one blasphemy after another issued from his lips, the black spittle ran down his chin. "Goddamn it all to hell!" He was screaming now, unleashing all his pent-up violence against his God above, below. "Goddamn it all to hell..."

The phone rang.

"Junkers…Junkers Implement. Yeah. Hi, Starky. What? Yeah. I got that—it's called—circle seven. When? 'Round three. I'll be in. No. I never leave." He hung up.

The call brought him back to his senses, but did nothing to lessen his anger. Extracting his hand from his coat pocket now, he produced the half-pint bottle he'd secured there the night before, just in case. He broke the seal then glanced at the clock; it was going on two—later than thought, after all.

Great flakes of flame fell slowly as snow on a windless day. Row after row of black portals filled with ash and cinders stared out at them. A handful of ash banked up around the frame trickled on its own into the steel tub on the floor, but the rest—a dozen tubfuls at least—would have to be scraped away with iron brushes.

Jim stood off to the side with one of the brushes in his hand. It was long as a lance, and it was tipped with steel bristles. He tapped it against the cement floor, an impatient knight's squire waiting to be of service. His father glanced back at him over the top of his glasses, grabbed the brush away and went to work. He pulled his mouth into a grimace as he poked the brush into each of the ports, his black teeth and blackened gums matching the blackness of the coal and the darkness of the shop, so that he looked completely at home in his frigid labor, wordlessly working away, his attendant ready with the next brush—a short one for use in close combat once the dragon was adequately subdued.

When the ash tub would hold no more they carted it off between them, each grabbing a handle; they moved slowly and awkwardly from the weight, then dumped it behind the shop in the trash pile. Broken belts and chains, tires, and odd bits of machinery poked out of the snow there, as if an enormous engine had fallen from the heavens and crashed, splintering into an unrecognizable heap.

Not a word passed between them except for Arly's occasional orders: "Move—tub over. Here, gimmie the short one. Take this…" Pile after pile of ash fell off into the tub; a fine, black dust filled the air, coating each of them as Arly worked away deeper and deeper into the bowels with the long brush and Jim scraped the sides clean with the short brush and scooped up the handfuls of dust that fell outside the tub.

It was twilight when they finished with the ashes. Arly turned on the shop lights. The bare bulbs dangled above them like darkly luminous spiders letting themselves down from the ceiling on black webs.

The last part of the job was to shovel the furnace full again, dumping scoop after scoop of coal into its bottomless belly. By the time they finished, it was completely dark out. Snow scraped against the shop windows and wind shook the massive panes.

Arly primed the furnace and they waited for all the burners to flame.

Deep inside the coals caught, and through the portals, fiery, newborn constellations burned orange and red. In two weeks they would haul them all out again—tubfuls of burnt up stars. Dead night.

"Tell your mother—goin' up to Nob's. Be home around ten, eleven."

Jim nodded.

"Tell her—got funeral, so better see…Naw. Just tell her, I'll eat up there."

Jim nodded again, already half-way out the door. He tucked his chin into his coat and headed home.

Arly went up to the office.

His greasy fingers in the till, he counted out the money there, then wound the bills into a roll, snapped a rubber band around it and dropped it into his pocket. He shut off all the lights, tripped the lock on the door and, pulling his hat down tightly against the snowy gusts, trailed off to Nobiskrugs. He knew he needed to make an appearance. After funerals it was the customary stop for everyone around.

There was hardly room to walk between the cars and pickups idling on the snow-packed street. White exhaust clouded into hovering pockets, trapped until another blast of wind tore them all away. There was only the white of the snow, the white of the exhaust, and the blackness of the sky above.

"Hey, Arly! Wha' dya say?"

"Earl." Arly nodded, setting his iced-over glasses on the bar top.

"'Nother blizzard, huh?"

"Looks like it, Earl."

"Yes sir. That's right. That is right."

Earl pounded the bar with the stump of his arm—the rest of it got chewed off by a sickle mower when he was a boy. "Frankie! A drink for the mayor and me!"

"Thanks, Earl."

Earl's half-arm went up in a salute. "Too bad about Charlie."

"Yeah. Too bad."

"Cigarettes, you know."

"Yeah. I know."

"I cut 'em out a long time ago myself. You used to smoke, didn't you?"

"Used to."

"You chew though."

"Yeah."

"That's not so bad."

"No."

"Guys gotta have somethin'."

"Yeah. I guess."

"You know, they only found out about six months ago."

"Charlie?"

"Yeah."

"Nothin' to do bout it. Just eats you right up."

"Yeah. It's bad stuff."

"Eats you right up. That is a fact. Only weighed eighty pounds when he died."

"That right?"

"Yes sir. That is a fact. That is a fact."

Frankie brought the drinks.

Earl slid his glass into his hand with a flick of his stump. "Here's to Charlie."

"Charlie," Arly echoed.

"Yeahp. Charlie Gaugn. Charlie *is gone* all right. That's a fact. That is a fact."

Earl emptied his glass and moved off, disappearing into the crowd.

Arly took a look around. Wirt was down at the end of the bar. Rum had warmed his voice into a theatrical resonance, and his hands cradled his belly in his customary pose as he regaled the crowd with the alcoholic nostalgia and wisdom of his profession.

"Old Fitz, Bobby, then what, a month back, Ole O'Leary. One burned, one smothered...I tell you, all you farmers would live a lot longer if you went into a slightly safer line of work. Hell, for as many of you as I'm seeing lately, you might as well join the army and go off to Viet Nam. My opinion is that you would increase your survival rate considerably."

His audience laughed, saluting him with their beers. He was a performer, and they liked the way he talked. He was extremely wealthy as well; his mansion on Lake Cocytus stuffed with antiques, his yearly trips to Europe, and his monthly trips to Chicago just to see the opera all combined to give him an exotic aura of culture and refinement. But he didn't hold himself aloof, everyone agreed.

"Yes, out of the whole bunch lately, old Red Leary is the only one that went natural—his heart just gave out."

"That's the best way," someone said.

"I imagine so," replied Wirt. "But truly, it's not how you die, it's how you live."

Beery nods of sentimental assent went flitting about the crowd as each bobbing listener drew up his own private calculations, the hurried tallies of which would prove they did know the secret of a life well-lived, and that even though their lives so far had not been what they wanted, all that would change now, and each mortal day left would be a living expression of truth and beauty, or what words passed for it, until a few more rounds taught them the same old fears, and they felt the rottenness of their flesh once again, the impossibility of their plight, and the certainty only of misery and horrible death.

Across the room, Earl was crazily flapping his arms as the punchline to some joke. Everyone around him laughed wildly.

Wirt drew himself up to his full height and headed out on a different tack. "If only we had the time, each one of us here should tell a story. We should just go right around the room, and it's too bad we can't do it, but I tell you what I think we'd discover. We'd discover that each one of us had something in common, that we had one essential dream in life that spoke to everyone in the same way."

"To get drunk and stay drunk!" Someone sang out, invoking a chorus of sputtering guffaws.

"And to get laid every night!" Another voice chimed, sending a second wave of knee-slapping laughter.

"Well, aside from that!" Wirt continued, laughing himself, and even doing a little dance as if he was delighted with the joke, because he always knew exactly what to do and what to say as he continued to work the crowd. The laughter subsided and he was in control of the situation once again.

"No, I think what we'd find out is that each of us," he paused, "That each of us is desperate and lost."

"Maybe so," Charlie Klamman sputtered in his shrill, gurgle of a voice, But what does that have to do with the price of beans?"

"Everything and nothing," Wirt replied, suddenly weakened. He was getting lost himself—he wanted to say something else. He was so close...Maybe the rum...The more he tried to organize his thoughts, the more scattered they became. It was useless. He had no right. The ghostly odor of formaldehyde filled his nostrils; he fumbled for his watch, gathered up his hat and coat, and with hurried apologies—long road to drive, bad weather—disappeared into the gloom.

"Never know he was the undertaker."

"No sir. He's different, but I like him. He sure can talk though. Shoulda been a preacher."

"Better'n what we got now."

"Christ, what a joke. Put me to sleep."

Arly watched the door close behind Wirt. He found himself watching the door for some time after as well, waiting.

He finished his drink and ordered another. He glanced over at the memorial jar for Charlie behind the bar.

Shoulda quit those things. His own damn fault. Used to hunt together when we were kids. Pheasants thick as a…Hell. Just a black cloud. All them others. It's their own fault too. Stupid mistakes. I don't know how many times I tell those guys.

He sat there drinking until the nine o'clock whistle blew. Still, she didn't show. Just when he was deciding to wait a while longer and have a couple more, the phone rang behind the bar. It was for him.

"Hello, Mayor."

"Hey, Kiddo. What's up?"

"Can't make it tonight. Goddamned Bob was gonna blow out the driveway, but he hasn't made it home yet. I don't know where he is. But the car's buried, I'm stranded, and that's that."

"That Bob…Can't one—your boys blow it out?"

"I don't know where they are either."

"You gonna be all right?"

"Oh yeah. I got plenty of wine to keep me warm!"

Arly laughed. "Well. Nothin' we can do 'bout it. Gimmie a call tomorrow. Lemme know what's goin' on."

"Sorry about this."

"Nah. You—stay warm."

He decided to have a couple more anyway. There was no sense going home yet. He signaled Frankie and threw a dollar on the bar. As he waited, he glanced over at Charlie's jar again.

Maybe shoulda gone. Don't know. Been what, four years? Yeah. Four years since dad. Christmas. So damn cold that year. Goin' back and forth, one hospital after another. Then Will. He was really torn up. Cried like a baby. That was bad. That was bad all right. Least the store's goin' good now. Just so mother don't monkey up the books. Gotta watch her like I don't know what. Like a hawk. Ten times a day, gotta yell at her about one thing or another. Makes me so damn mad sometimes…Yeah. Charlie. That's a shame. Drive all the way to Madrid for groceries now. No one's gonna take over *that* piece of junk. Sure let it go to the dogs. His dad kept it up good. Charlie just didn't have…well, just too bad.

Hour after hour his thoughts kept circling the same rounds. Periodically someone would buy him a drink and he would reciprocate, in the process exchanging a few guarded statements about weather and market conditions. However, by midnight he could barely speak, and it was time to go home.

The sky had cleared and the stars shone down brilliantly. He cursed as he glanced up at them—no cloud cover—only get colder and colder now.

The pickup barely turned over. He should have gone out and started it earlier. He was afraid he might have to walk, then the engine finally grabbed. He waited a good five minutes for it to run smoothly, then inched off, tires squeaking through the packed ruts.

With the snow piled high as the cab on both sides of the street he felt like he was crawling through a tunnel, and as he navigated from one end of town to the other on the three block drive home, he shivered uncontrollably, and he cursed aloud at the storms and the cold, his gloved hands clutching the wheel as he peered into the tiny spot on the windshield—about the size of a quarter—that the defroster had managed to keep clear.

He turned into the driveway and killed the engine. The house was dark. She was asleep. He could have a couple more.

He settled into his chair and poured himself a glass. All the stations were off the air so he just sat there staring into space. The cold drive had sobered him considerably, and it seemed as if the more he drank now the more sober he became, until he finally passed out.

Around two, he was startled awake again by the wind crashing against the house. He staggered up to the drapes and pulled them aside.

The stars were blotted out along with everything else. The clouds had moved in after all. The blizzard was in full force.

He stared into the consuming, whorling whiteness, shapes there dancing up raggedly out of the dark. Hypnotic squalls drawing him deeply into their trance, he stared, clutching the drapes in his clenched fists, his teeth set. He cursed, though softly to himself now, over and over, circling through the same blasphemous rounds from which he could find no exit, from which there was no exit.

Chapter Eighteen

Nora pulled the afghan around her shoulders and peered out the window. Soft ashen snow was falling in the street.

"You have deprived me of my friends."

She smiled. "Made me repulsive to them, imprisoned, with no escape; my eyes are worn out with suffering."

She would go see Father Misere…"You know what the church proscribes in these situations. You're raising three fine young Catholic boys…"

But she no longer had the strength or desire to love, least of all to love the God who made her only to endure through the motions of a counterfeit life. Bitterness washed over her like the sea. She had been lost, given up, left alone among the dead. She smiled again.

Life among the dead. Punishment for what crime? There had been no crime. A poor choice. Circumstances. The sea washes over these bones, and that is all.

It was impossible to speak. It was forbidden to speak…

"Went over—priest's."

"She always over there?"

"Jus' 'bout."

"Got a rival, then!"

"Hell. Sometimes—think—he can have her. Get so damn tired…"

"What's her problem anyway?"

"Cryin'—mopin' around…"

"Gotta wear on a person."

"Tell you, it does."

"What are you gonna do?"

"Don't know. What I'd like—do, just take off. Just get in the car and drive."

"Gonna take me with?"

"Sure—You come with! We'll just drive off. Say—hell with everything! We need money—we'll stop—pick raspberries or something!"

"Raspberries! You're funny!"

"Maybe rob banks too!"

"Now you're talkin'!"

"You know, when I was—boy, used—travel all around the country with my dad. California. Mexico. Florida. Saw everything! Saw—twice over, some of it. Took—dog along too—had a dog then. Me, my brother, sister, Mom, Dad. Roads weren't too good then neither. No interstate."

"Sounds like quite an adventure."

"It was. Yeah. Yes ma'am it was."

"You don't go anyplace anymore, do you?"

"No. No I don't."

"Well, you're right then! We should both of us just take off! Hell! Bob wouldn't even know I was gone! He's just a ghost anyway. Where do you want to go first?"

"That's easy! South. Straight south where—good and hot!"

"You always like it down south."

"Well…"

"Good and hot…"

"You…"

She tipped her wine glass to him and winked. They laughed, then she slapped her hand on the bar top and ordered another round.

He spit, then poked another pinch of snuff into his mouth."It's no good though."

"What?"

"No good thinkin' that way."

"What way?"

"You know. Jokin' about leavin."

"Well, yeah…But we were just joking. No harm in that."

"No but…Just no good."

"Okay then, we won't joke about it no more. I just thought since you started it…"

"I didn't say I didn't start it! Just don't want to talk about it."

"Okay then."

"Sometimes maybe—just think it's a good idea—you don't stick your nose into my business."

"I didn't stick my nose in your business!"

"You know what I mean."

"No I don't! I didn't stick my nose anywhere! We were just talking here, then all of a…"

"Just drop it."

"Okay, Okay. Somebody got up on the wrong side this morning."

"I just don't…"

He fell silent, finished his drink and waved for another round.

"Maybe I shouldn't be sticking around here tonight," She said.

"No. You stick around. Lonely."

"Okay. How are the boys?"

"I don't know. Jake's got some crazy…Well, now he's goin'—school—be a writer. He's gettin'…I don't know. Tip though, he's thinkin' engineering. That's a good plan, I think."

"Lot's of money in that."

"Yes. Yes there is."

"How about your youngest then?"

"He's—freshman this year. Don't know. Awful quiet. I'm afraid about that. Gonna have trouble. Was in a play though. He might—we're thinkin' maybe trade school over—Seneca. Grades aren't too…Well…Always knew about that though."

"That's too bad. Mine…He's his old man all over again."

She finished her wine and called for another round. "Your boy, he'll do all right. He's just a kid now."

"Hope so."

"Still windy out there, huh?"

"Yeah. Still blowin' pretty bad."

The drinks came.

"I been…I been thinkin'," he said.

"Yeah?"

"Maybe…"

"Maybe what?"

"Maybe this isn't such a good idea."

"What?"

"This…You know…All this."

"I don't know what the hell you're talking about."

"You and me. I'm talking about you and me."

"Where'd all this come from?"

"Well, it's…She's sick."

"Who? Who's sick?"

"Nora. She sick she's got…They don't know…maybe…That's why she's not…"

"Why didn't you tell me?"

"Well, might not be anything."

"Why didn't you tell me anyway? Is that why she's been going over to the priest all the time?"

"I don't know. I suppose."

"Well, why didn't you tell me? I'm sorry."

"So I, I just don't think…"

"Sure, I understand. That why you've been…Well."

"Might not be anything."

"When are they gonna find out?"

"Week, maybe."

"You should go home to her right now."

"I suppose I should."

"Right now."

"I'll. I'll call you."

"Don't worry about me."

He decided to leave the pickup parked by the store and walk home instead. It was nearly midnight. He gripped his hat in his hand and pressed it against his side as he bent into the wind.

He couldn't remember the last time he'd actually been out walking at this hour—he always drove. Tree branches danced wildly around him and above him, casting their shadows on the road in a hazy blue light.

No. It wasn't right. Not now at least…

Chapter Nineteen

Something hadn't been right for a long time—almost a month now. Doctor Schadow said it was nothing to worry about, but it wouldn't hurt to run some tests; his voice was reassuring, but Nora saw the hollow smile on his face. Now the results were back, and on the phone the receptionist said she should come in soon as possible.

Was it always this way? She thought as she turned onto highway 13 and headed east to Seneca. It's probably nothing. Doubt was good. She knew what the truth was about everything, but it always helped to think otherwise, and to think that she might be wrong. What she feared most was losing the strength to doubt.

Her thoughts ran on, careful to avoid certain words that were especially poisonous; when she got close to them she would veer off because there was no sense thinking them when you weren't sure. And how could anyone ever be sure about anything? Nobody knew anything. What if everything in the world turned out to be a lie? Or maybe everything wasn't even here in the first place, so nothing mattered. But I'm in this car, I'm alive...I'm driving to the doctor's office. The office might not even be there anymore. When I get there nothing will be there. Why would the doctor's office have to be there in the first place? Just because it was there once doesn't mean it has to be there again.

She passed the drive-in on the edge of town. Three ragged holes gaped in the screen from the last wind storm. Half the letters on the marquee had been ripped away leaving only *Beyond…Valley of…*The screen always reminded her of an enormous sail, especially in the wintertime.

The waiting room was bathed in a dull yellow light and it was tiny as a cupboard; it had only three chairs crowded next to an oversized coffee table that took up half the floor. The table was strewn with greasy, dog-eared *Women's Home Companion's* and *Women's Journal's*.

"Mrs. Kern?"

"Yes?"

"The doctor will see you now."

The nurse led her down a long hallway barely wide enough for two people to pass. The hallway had the same yellow light as the waiting room, only less of it.

The nurse told Nora to sit on the examining table, her hand vaguely motioning toward it from the door, then she closed the door and left.

Nora folded her hands in her lap to keep them from trembling. This would be how it would be. This would be how it would begin. And how it would begin. And then it would end. And then it would end. This is how it would begin to end. How it would be. It would begin. He is not here. There is no one here. When I was little and everyone was dead…Left alone among the dead. Wretched…

Doctor Schadow's face was molded from a dark wax, and the skin drooped under his eyes as if the wax had melted once, then hardened again, leaving permanent tears. He set his clipboard on the tiny metal desk in the corner, sat down in the metal chair next to the desk and crossed his skeleton legs. He lifted his face, the carved illusion of long suffering in his eyes peering up at Nora, who had not moved an inch since he came into the room.

"Hello, Nora," He finally managed to say. "How are you feeling?"

"Fine. Well…"

"I know." He paused, his hand going up distractedly as if it was meant comfort her. "The results are back." He took up his clipboard, opened the cover then closed it again.

Nora felt her body in flames. He was still looking at her, but he didn't say anything. She felt as if he was studying her, still looking for something to complete his examination. As if they hadn't already found out enough to torment me...

"But let me remind you," He finally said, "That these results still aren't conclusive, at least not as conclusive as we'd like them to be. You know, of course, that it's important to be absolutely certain in these cases. So again, it's not conclusive, that is, we need to run one more test with another lab, just to verify—to have a second opinion that is. But, based on your symptoms and on the results of the tests so far, it's safe to say that in all likelihood you probably do have cancer. Colon cancer, as we suspected."

Each new reservation and new qualification at least had the effect of so infuriating Nora that she forgot for a moment about the deadly seriousness of her worst fear, but when her fear returned, it was with a numbing force; the word "cancer" like a tremendous, leveling wind, gathering itself up out of all the desolate waste, in one shattering blow stripped the life from her limbs.

She saw his mouth continue to move as he read down his list of rehearsed platitudes, but she had already moved far away from his world—it was petty enough to begin with, but now it was becoming ludicrous, rotten, hypocritical, lying...

Her head was swirling —he'd call tomorrow and let her know for sure—the results—arrangements for the clinic in Rochester—she sensed the same useless smile in the wax, the waxen voice, stupid words...then somehow she managed to find her way out of the office and down the two flights of black wooden stairs, the handrail feeling strangely hot—so hot she couldn't touch it, then as she pulled her hand away she lost her balance, started to fall.

She clutched her purse and the next thing she knew she was out on the street, her eyes watering in the blinding light; she stumbled along deliriously, the hot wind on her face. There were no buildings, no sidewalk, no streets…only an empty desert there. It was all that had ever been there. She lived her life in a wasteland, and now she would die in the same wasteland.

He was good at keeping his secret from me, but he couldn't keep it forever—he knew it all along, the instant I told him he knew—but they always have to lie, and now they're going to try and cut it out of me. One more test. Why? I already know what's growing inside of me. They can't tell me what I already know, what I already feel in my own body. It's death there. It's a little speck of death and it grows bigger every day. It's my punishment. It's my punishment for being stupid, for not getting out when I could, for not living, and now it's too late. Everything is too late.

Slowly she became aware of the other people on the sidewalk, each face filling her with disgust and anger. Petty, stupid lives. Do they know anything? No. They're all ignorant. They're all lying to themselves…

But still he said he really didn't know for sure…Maybe…It's true, maybe he was being honest with me, letting me know exactly what was going on. He did have the results from one test and he needed to tell me. It's just one test. If it would have come back negative maybe they wouldn't have run another test, and then the first test might have been wrong, and I actually did have it, but then it wouldn't have been detected, and that would even be worse because who knows…And then if they run two tests, and at first I thought I didn't have it, and then find out that I did…No. I'd rather have it this way. There's a reason they check these things. If it's just a bad scare then that's that…

She laughed, then caught a reflection of herself in a store window and suddenly felt faint; the rush of contradictions and frenzied rationalizations continued their agonizing course unchecked. She didn't feel as if she was even walking on solid ground, and the heat…

There was a little restaurant called Clem's she liked to go to just around the corner. It was air-conditioned and the booths in back were especially dark and cool. As she waited to cross the street she stared up at the familiar red neon hand waving brokenly above the door.

A pick-up drove by, heaped with black tangles of barbed wire that looked like the nest of some enormous rusting bird. Then, an especially strong gust of wind blew up, and as she turned her head to shield her eyes she noticed for the first time a shriveled old woman standing beside her. It was as if she glided there out of nowhere. The woman had black stains in the flesh across her forehead and down her cheek. She had a dowager's hump and she was clutching a torn paper sack. She smiled up at Nora, her mouth twisting as if she was trying to speak, but nothing came out.

The heavy wooden door slammed behind her and a familiar waitress glanced up from the counter, then lowered her eyes again to her work, sorting silverware into a plastic tray. Nora took a booth against the back wall, drinking in the cool air, and for a moment she was able to take refuge in the old associations she had with the ordinary objects around her—napkin holders, salt shakers, the green lamps on the wall, the whirring black fans above—and she was able to forget, but not for long, because these talisman's in no time seemed to turn on her and to mock her with their changelessness and their artificial and useless immortality. A nauseating wave flooded over her and she felt herself falling deeper and deeper under it, unable to breath, then remembering that a moment before she had smiled, the memory of that smile also turned on her and mocked her: didn't she know? She would die now, and that would be that.

Another test won't change it. Just let me die so at least I won't have to think anymore or be afraid anymore. It's not fair to have to think. Why do I have to think?

So, God, you've made a fool of me. Just when I thought I could get out again...Now, what's the point? You've given me life and I've thrown it away—you're right. I deserve this. It's my punishment, and I deserve it. All the things you gave me and all the things I could have had...Now I know exactly what's going to happen. Sarah Faul, Margie Black and now...This is what you get. First they bury you six feet deep...

Buried alive, then buried dead. Three years? Four years? Sarah's had it two years. Margie just got it. Hair's gone already. Skeleton.

The waitress clicked her ball point. She had been standing beside the table for some time. Nora reached for the menu tucked behind the napkin dispenser. "Just give me a few more minutes."

The waitress swirled a damp rag over the table top and left.

Nora stared blankly at the menu, the flush of shame reddening her face. She didn't want to be seen, and why she even bothered coming to the cafe in the first place was becoming a greater and greater mystery to her. Another time she would linger an hour or more over coffee, imagining conversations with a friend.

The smell of dust was everywhere, and the few cars that drove through the wide, empty street made the town seem even more desolate. She walked along the sidewalk, no longer even trying to shield her face from the wind. The stores were deserted. No one bothered coming here anymore.

She drove home with all the windows open in the car. The trees that should be on the horizon were shrouded in dust, and the late afternoon sun was baking the fields; ever-receding mirages of rippling water beckoned her down the miles and miles of black pavement. She tried to listen to the radio, but it was impossible to hear anything in all the wind.

"So—what'd you find out?"

Nora looked vacantly through the window into the yard. It was shady under the trees. She wasn't sure if she heard Arly's voice or not. She'd called him on the phone and told him she was back, and now he seemed to be standing there, in the kitchen, drinking a glass of water, but everything was so far away that she couldn't be certain—was he there or not? If he wasn't there, would it make any difference? Her green eyes were starting to water and she held her folded hands tightly against her stomach.

"They're going to run another test. The doctor will call me tomorrow."

"What—they think it is?"

She didn't answer.

He took a step toward her. "So—they gonna run 'nother test you say?"

"Yes."

"Well—how you feel?"

"How do you think I feel?" She turned her head and stared at him. As soon as he saw her eyes he looked down at the floor and walked absently away, then half-turned toward her again and spoke.

"Maybe—should lie down."

"I don't know what I should do."

"Well—gonna be another test…"

They were both silent.

"Why don't—lie down?" He repeated with the jerk of his hand, his thumb pointing the way to the bedroom. "I got—meeting tonight. Town board. Seven o'clock. Maybe I shouldn't go though…"

"I don't care."

"Gonna talk about—new sewer so, kind of important."

She gave an indifferent wave of her hand past her face.

He started back to the kitchen, then turned. "Need anything?"

"No."

"Better rest then. I'll eat up there. Always got ham or somethin'".

He left. She continued staring out the window for a long time, then sat down at her desk in the back of the living room. She opened her Bible and read, and even though she couldn't concentrate on any of the words, she kept turning the pages until it was dark, then she closed the book, laid her head down on it and wept.

She had never felt so utterly and completely alone. The wind blew unabated.

She opened her Bible again, turned to Psalm 88 and read aloud, her lamp casting the shadow of her bowed head against the white wall. "Yahweh, God of my salvation, when I cry out to you in the night, may my prayer reach your presence, hear my cry for help." She paused, feeling each word now resonate within her being, then continued again. "For I am filled with misery, my life is on the brink of Sheol; already numbered among those who sink into oblivion, I am as one bereft of strength, left alone among the dead, like the slaughtered lying in the grave, whom you remember no more, cut off as they are from your protection."

The bitterness in the words was the only companion she had to her own bitterness, and she drank it down, gathering strength from it. "You have plunged me to the bottom of the grave, in the darkness, in the depths; weighted down by your anger, kept low by your waves. You have deprived me of my friends, made me repulsive to them, imprisoned, with no escape; my eyes are worn out with suffering. I call to you, Yahweh, all day, I stretch out my hands to you.

"Do you work wonders for the dead, can shadows rise up to praise you? Do they speak in the grave of your faithful love, of your constancy in the place of perdition? Are your wonders known in the darkness, your saving justice in the land of oblivion?

"But, for my part, I cry to you, Yahweh, every morning my prayer comes before you; why, Yahweh, do you rebuff me, turn your face away from me? Wretched and close to death since childhood, I have borne your terrors—I am finished! Your anger has overwhelmed me, your terrors annihilated me. They flood around me all day long, close in on me all at once. You have deprived me of friends and companions, and all that I know is the dark."

She looked up from the page, suddenly exhausted, but filled with a sense of obscure triumph. To live, to suffer and to die. To live is to suffer and die. That was the only truth. Flesh is here to feel pain, and we're trapped in it until it rots away from us. All flesh is pain. If I suffer, it is only because I am alive. If I am to suffer, I am to suffer. It is the only truth.

Arly still wasn't home. She wasn't surprised either; most likely he wouldn't be out as late as usual though—he was still capable of going through certain motions of sensitivity—and at least he probably wouldn't even try to touch her tonight.

She was so tired she could barely stand, and all she wanted now was to get to bed and sleep. She ran her hand across the page of the open

Bible, turned the lamp off, then dragged herself to her room, pulled the covers back and laid her head on her pillow.

She snapped her bedside light off and closed her eyes. She was asleep immediately, but suddenly, after only a few seconds, her eyes opened wide again as if an electric shock went through her. She screamed aloud, "And God be damned!"

The words were out of her before she could think. She laid there staring fixedly into the dark, her heart beating madly, the wind still crashing in waves against the house.

Chapter Twenty

For an entire week now the wind had been blowing; dust devils cut over the black September fields and danced straight through town, doors banging in their wake, ghost fingers prying open every lock, shaking every window.

The usual late afternoon collection of pickups was pulled up in front of Nob's bar; every once in a while a grain truck rumbled down the street on its way to the elevator. The only living soul to be seen was Herb Tote enthroned as always on the paintless bench outside of his garage. A grease-smeared, silent idol between two antique gas pumps that haven't been used in twenty years, he surveyed the progress of the dust.

Jim was sitting on one of the steel chairs by the front window in his father's store, himself staring into the street and the dust. His father was in the office. Will was behind the counter, scratching down numbers on a pad in a cloud of cigarette smoke.

Jim had been waiting longer than usual for his father to give his orders—always the first thing to greet him after school—but the orders were still forthcoming, and something else was different today, more than could be explained by the menace of the wind which always seemed to throw things off. It was silent as usual, but it was an especially portentous silence.

For a long time this type of silence had been gathering: weeks, months, years...It had grown subtly and not so subtly. It was in the land and in the bones, a dimension unto itself, taken for granted like the dimensions of space or time. Then, simultaneously obliterating and amplifying that silence, the phone rang. It was the call the silence had been waiting for, the dust had been waiting for.

Jim heard his father's voice but could not make out the words; then, the cry of a beast dormant for ages in a forgotten pit, now waking, a strange inhuman sobbing welled up.

Not knowing which instinct to obey, to run *from* the sound or to run *to* it, Jim stood trancelike as his father came lunging toward him, weaving drunkenly, his hat crushed in his hand, then tore past his son like he wasn't even there. The screen door slammed. Will called out to Jim.

"You better go with your father!"

"What?"

"Just go. Go on. He's goin' home!"

"What?"

"Just go!"

Arly flooded the pickup in his race to get home so he had to floor the footfeed to get the engine going, and when it finally caught he popped the clutch, tearing off just as Jim jumped in and pulled the door shut.

Arly's mouth gnawed wordlessly at the air; Jim could ask, but there would be no answer, and as everything around him took on a bizarre clarity and significance, his senses were being sharpened by the sensation of uncomprehending terror.

He couldn't look at his father whose face had become too strange and grotesque, so looking the other way out the passenger window he caught a glimpse of Herb Tote on his bench who, with a slow, grizzled pivot of his head, followed the pickup as they tore off, wheels kicking up the dust. Jim studied every detail as the spidery old man plunged a hairy fist into his overall pocket, ripped a leaf off his Red Man and worked it into his mouth, the black juice running down his chin.

Arly could barely keep the pickup out of the ditch as he aimed down the driveway by the house, then he killed the engine and jumped out while the truck was still rolling. By the time it finally came to a stop halfway into the lawn he was diving drunkenly down the sidewalk. Jim was still in the cab.

The wind tore at the brown leaves on the trees and sent them whirling in the dust, mixing them with bits of trash. For a long time Jim sat watching it all—how the leaves swirled around him, how the trees bent in the wind, their branches clacking against one another. The pickup smelled of dry hay and Will's cigarettes. A black cloud of flies buzzed in the dust.

He felt as if he could stay there for a hundred years and nothing would change. He still wouldn't know what to do: to run toward the house and all its terror and pain, and had nothing more to offer now than some new, as yet, unnamed terror and some new, as yet, ambiguous pain, or to stay away, to save himself.

He took a deep breath and got out. As he walked he thought of himself watching himself from far away, recording everything that was taking place: his hand sheltering his eyes, how the wind cut through his clothes. It was the only way things could be now. He had suspected it for a long time, and now he knew.

Nora was still holding the telephone in her hand. Arly was embracing her awkwardly from the side. Her arms were limp. Her eyes were black hollows; all their light had disappeared.

Jim stood at the door watching them. Not a word was said. They were in their own world and he was in his. It was impossible to say how much time passed that way.

Later that night, after dark, his father would finally explain. "Your mother has to have—operation—Rochester. You're gonna have to stay at Grandma's."

Arly didn't use the word "cancer." He didn't know how to use words like that. Maybe he felt that if he didn't speak them, bad things wouldn't happen. But that night he didn't use it because he didn't think it was necessary. It was his way of protecting Jim.

The word came the next day. Nora and Jim were at the kitchen table. They would be leaving shortly after Jim got on the high-school bus for Madrid. She raised her coffee cup to her mouth, then lowered it again. "Your mother has cancer. Do you know that?" She stopped, then stared down at her cup. After a long silence, she added. "They're going to cut it out, and then I'm coming back…"

But all that would come later. The only thing he knew as he stood at the door looking at them was that something had changed forever. There had been a phone call and everything changed. He began to feel awkward and ashamed as he watched them in their wordless embrace; he knew instinctively that he would have to wait for an explanation, and since, again, he could not form the words to ask what was wrong, he crept away from the door, turned his back to them, and stared out the porch window.

There was the plastic click of the receiver set back in its cradle, then his parents went into their bedroom and closed the door. Nora wept, soft and muffled at first, her face buried in her pillow, but soon deep sobs welled up interspersed with long, horrible silences, and as the sobbing became increasingly bitter Jim could take no more and left the house.

Outside, the wind tore away her voice and he sat down beside a tree, lost in his own thoughts, staring up at the sky. A gray haze hung everywhere. There were no clouds, only darker and lighter shades of ash. Sparrows were picking at the ground around him, gray flecks on the brown grass.

He didn't know how he was supposed to feel. He thought of different ways, but nothing made sense. He closed his eyes tightly and cleared his thoughts once again, then he stared into the endless gray sky as if seeking the right answer there, but nothing came of it, and he finally gave up and wandered aimlessly around the town. He had some ideas, but they puzzled him, and it wasn't until the next day, after the word was finally uttered and after he said good-bye to his mother at the breakfast table, that he finally began to confirm the suspicions about the thoughts he had been having.

The instant he heard her say the word he knew what it meant, and he also knew instinctively that its true meaning could never be uttered. When you had cancer, you died. That was the meaning of the word. It was the only definition. There would be operations, and then she would die.

He wondered if he loved his mother. His instinct could define cancer but not love. He felt sad for her. He knew that. He knew she was trapped, and he could even forgive her for treating him the way she had—it was because she was unhappy. That much he could see. She had been cheated, and now she was being cheated again.

But the feeling that frightened him most was that he was happy. Now that the word had been used he knew for certain. Her cancer was giving him an eerie sense of freedom which separated him from everyone and everything else in the world.

He smiled to himself and looked around at the others on the bus. The ugly voices jabbering around him no longer filled him with the old sense of disgust; he pitied them now. They would be left behind. He was seeing what had always been there. Her cancer was the confirmation that he would escape from all the ugliness that surrounded him. He would get out. He would not die there or become like them because she was going to die for him.

The bus turned onto mainstreet, and as it drove past the store he saw his father heading for his pickup. He was coming down the sidewalk. The weeds that grew waist high on both sides of the walk twisted left and right in the wind.

They would be leaving for Rochester in a few minutes. He had to go to the store first to take care of a few things—they'd be gone for a week, longer than he'd ever been away. He was afraid Will wouldn't be able to take care of things on his own.

As usual, he walked with his head bowed low. Jim remembered the day the two of them were crossing the street from the cafe when suddenly his father scooped a quarter from the pavement and held it up in the air for Jim to inspect. "Always pays—keep your eyes to the ground!"

Jim sensed it was supposed to be a joke, but it somehow didn't come off.

Just before the bus left town, Jim got yet another look at old Herb Tote who appeared suddenly from out of the gaping darkness of his shop like a spider frightened from its den. Herb peered blankly at the passing bus, then settled into his bench to tally up another day in Junkers, North Dakota, his mental ledger recording all entrances and exits, and the implications thereof.

In about an hour he would be watching Arly and Nora leave. He would know by the end of the day what it was all about. The word "cancer" would come murmuring up out of the dust, then settle back ultimately to live there again forever in all the silent, dark corners of town, doing more to define those corners than any other single word could.

The bus headed off into the country. Jim stared out the window at the black fields and the gray clouds.

He watched a flock of ravens rise up and lift raggedly into the sky.

About the Author

Paul Jentz teaches English at Anoka-Ramsey Community College in Minnesota. He is currently at work on another novel about Junkers, North Dakota.

9 780595 169573